D1369840

LIFE-PRESERVER

LIFE-PRESERVER

James Pattinson

Chivers Press • **G.K. Hall & Co.**
Bath, England **Waterville, Maine USA**

This Large Print edition is published by Chivers Press, England, and by G.K. Hall & Co., USA.

Published in 2001 in the U.K. by arrangement with Robert Hale Limited.

Published in 2001 in the U.S. by arrangement with Robert Hale Limited.

U.K. Hardcover   ISBN 0-7540-4659-1   (Chivers Large Print)
U.K. Softcover   ISBN 0-7540-4660-5   (Camden Large Print)
U.S. Softcover   ISBN 0-7838-9597-6   (Nightingale Series Edition)

The text of this Large Print edition is unabridged.
Other aspects of the book may vary from the original edition.

Set in 16 pt. New Times Roman.

Printed in Great Britain on acid-free paper.

British Library Cataloguing in Publication Data available

Library of Congress Cataloging-in-Publication Data

Pattinson, James, 1915–
    Life-preserver / James Pattinson.
      p.   cm.
    ISBN 0-7838-9597-6 (lg. print : sc : alk. paper)
    1. Central Americans—Fiction. 2. Heads of state—Fiction.
    3. Photographers—Fiction. 4. Exiles—Fiction. 5. Large type
    books. I. Title.
    PR6066.A877 L55 2001
    823'.914—dc21   2001039333

CONTENTS

CHAPTER ONE

FLIGHT

President Harrera was stuffing the last of the documents into the briefcase on his desk when he heard someone give a knock on the door of the room. It was the kind of knock which might have been made by a man who felt that he had no time to waste; there was a suggestion of impatience about it; and indeed before the president could utter a word of invitation the door was thrust open and Colonel Rias walked in. There was no mistaking the urgency in his manner, which he was making no attempt to disguise.

'You are ready, Señor Presidente?'

Harrera closed the briefcase, locked it and dropped the key into his pocket.

'I am ready.'

'Then I suggest we leave without further delay.'

The colonel spoke brusquely; it sounded more like an order than a suggestion, but Harrera took no offence; he had known Rias for practically all the fifty-two years of his life and there was no other man whom he would have trusted as implicitly as this tough, lean-faced soldier. And in fact, if it had not been for Rias he might never have had warning of the plot to assassinate him and take over the government by a military coup. His immediate impulse had been to move against the conspirators, but Rias had convinced him that there was no likelihood of any such measures being successful; the planned coup had powerful support in the armed services and resistance would merely have led to a futile shedding of blood.

Harrera had listened to Rias's argument and had bowed to the inevitable, not without a certain feeling of relief. The plain fact was that things had not been going well for the elected government of which he was the head. Indeed, the country was economically in dire straits. Perhaps it had been too much to expect that after centuries of dictatorial right-wing rule a moderate democratic régime could be successful in coping with all the complicated financial problems with which it was confronted. Striving to occupy the middle ground it failed to gain financial support either from the capitalist or the communist powers.

Cold-shouldered by both Russia and the United States, it was unable to obtain the credits it so desperately needed to enable it to carry out the reforms it had promised in its manifesto. To Harrera it had become all too obvious that good intentions were not enough; without money nothing could be done. They had been opposed by the wealthy land-owners from the start; soon they were losing the support of the disillusioned poor. It was a situation that appeared to be getting steadily worse and he could foresee no hope of improvement. Perhaps for this small Central American republic there was no hope.

There was of course something distasteful to him in the thought of running away; for that was what it amounted to. Was it not a cowardly thing to do? Perhaps. But what sense would there have been in sacrificing his own life for a lost cause? Nothing would have been gained by such a futile gesture.

And besides, there was Margarita to think about. It was ten years since Harrera's wife had died, but their daughter still lived as a constant reminder of her mother's beauty. The girl was twenty now, black-haired, dark-eyed and altogether delightful. Even the hard-bitten Colonel Rias was defenceless against the charms of the president's lovely daughter, and Harrera himself, though outwardly cold and undemonstrative, had a deep regard for her. So for her sake if for no other reason he felt compelled to take the prudent course and leave the country while there was yet time, taking her with him to the safety of some less volatile part of the world.

With the briefcase in his left hand and with Rias leading the way he left the room where so many of his recent working hours had been spent in dealing with the affairs of state which would no longer be any concern of his, giving a sigh of regret as he closed the door behind him. He had entered that room for the first time with such great hopes, but they had come to nothing; he had not succeeded in what he had set out to do; this fact, however unpalatable, could not be denied. As president of the republic he, Carlos Harrera, had been a failure.

Yet it should not have been so. He had done nothing wrong; he had done all that any man could have done; he had deserved a better fate, but there had been too much going against him. It was all so unfair; but when had fairness ever been a factor in public life? Money and guns were what counted, and he had had neither; at least not in sufficient quantity.

'Come,' Rias said, again with that note of urgency in his voice. 'There is no time to lose. The car is waiting.'

It was not, however, at the front of the imposing building with its facade of white stone which was the presidential palace, but in a quiet side-street at the rear. The time was long past midnight and the two men made their way quickly through the deserted corridors and out into the cool night air, having encountered no one on the way.

The large black limousine was parked unobtrusively in the shadow of a tree where the light from the nearest street-lamp scarcely reached it. The driver saw them coming, and

4

he got out and opened the rear door without saying a word. Harrera saw that Margarita was already seated inside, and he got in beside her. Rias climbed into the front with the driver, and the car moved smoothly away.

Harrera felt his daughter's hand touch his arm, and his instinctive reaction was to draw the arm away, as though shrinking from the intimacy of the gesture.

'You are all right, Papa?'

'I am ashamed,' Harrera said. It was a hole-and-corner business and he detested it. 'I am deserting my post. It is a despicable thing to do.'

'You must not blame yourself. You have done your best.'

'And the best was not enough.'

'No man could have done more. Perhaps there will come a time when you will return. Perhaps they will find they need you after all.'

Harrera answered with a touch of asperity: 'That day will never come. If you believe it you are deluding yourself. I have no illusions; when I have left this country there will be no possibility of a return, ever; it will be a permanent exile.'

'Even that may not be so very bad. You will be able to live in peace.'

'If I am allowed to do so.'

'You think you may not be?' She sounded concerned. 'You think someone may be sent to—'

'To kill me? Do not be afraid to say it. You must know they would very much prefer me to be dead than living in exile; they would feel safer. But do not worry yourself; it will not come to that. I shall be careful.'

She was not convinced that being careful would ensure his safety, but she did not pursue the subject. They fell silent as the black car, travelling at a speed that was only marginally below the level of recklessness and reflected the urgency of the journey, threaded its way through the narrow streets of the old city and out on to the road that would take them past the shanty town on the outer fringes and into the open country to the south. Once on this road the driver accelerated, the headlamps forcing a tunnel of light through the enveloping darkness as though cutting out a path for the car to follow.

Margarita was aware of a nervous flutter in the stomach, and though she tried to convince herself that there was no reason to suppose that everything would not go smoothly she could not avoid the feeling that something might yet occur to prevent their escape. Suppose the plan had been discovered; suppose someone had betrayed them.

Few people had any knowledge of what was afoot, but it needed no more than one of those few to utter a word or two in certain places, the merest whispered hint perhaps, and all would be put in jeopardy.

But it was unlikely. Colonel Rias had made the arrangements and he would have known whom he could trust. She herself had been told nothing until almost the last moment, and she knew only that a plane would be waiting for them, not at the airport but at some private airfield which lay at a distance of forty-odd kilometres from the capital city. This plane would fly them out of the country, and Rias would come with them, since it was certain that he would be arrested if he were to stay behind. To help Harrera he had forfeited his own safety.

To what country her father intended eventually to go she had not been told; for some reason he had been less than forthcoming on that point. She had a feeling that he still regarded her in some ways as a child and believed it was unnecessary, and perhaps even inadvisable, to give her his entire confidence. Which was quite ridiculous, of course; she would know eventually what their destination was, so what harm could there have been in telling her at once?

And as to being a child, a girl of twenty was hardly that; except perhaps in the eyes of a parent who with regard to domestic affairs was inclined to take a somewhat old-fashioned attitude.

Harrera suffered, she thought, from a lack of that humanising influence which only her mother had ever been able to exert. Since her

7

death he had become colder, more rigid in his ways. She believed he loved her, as she loved him, but it was apparent that he had difficulty in expressing his feeling. Essentially he was a shy man; with her no less than with other people. She knew that he would have been embarrassed if she had been too demonstrative in her behaviour towards him; therefore she maintained a certain reserve which was not a true reflection of her character.

Rias turned his head and spoke to the driver. He kept his voice low, and Margarita was unable to catch the drift of what he was saying, though she thought he addressed the man as 'Sergeant.' So it appeared that the driver was a soldier, although he was not in uniform. He had crisp black hair and was wearing a scuffed leather jacket fastened with a zipper. He looked tough.

He answered briefly: 'Yes, Colonel.' He did not take his eyes off the road, which was rough in places and full of twists. With the car travelling at such a speed it was essential that he should not allow his attention to be distracted from his driving.

They came to a village. There were no lights showing in the houses; apparently everyone was in bed. Starkly revealed in the glare of the headlamps, the white walls flickered past like ghosts, and a solitary dog slunk away down a side-turning as though aware of being caught in some nocturnal misdemeanour.

The police were waiting at the end of the village. The road made a snaking bend between the houses, and the driver was forced to reduce the speed. As he came out of the bend he saw the roadblock and stood hard on the brake pedal, cursing as he did so. There was a screech of tyres and the car skidded to a halt, almost throwing Harrera and his daughter from their seats.

'What is this?' Harrera said. 'What is going on here?'

Rias answered quickly: 'It is trouble, I think. Be calm and leave the talking to me. And you, Sergeant, do nothing unless I give the order. You understand?'

'Yes, Colonel.'

Margarita wondered just what the sergeant might do if Rias did give the order. Something violent perhaps? She prayed that it would not come to that. As far as she could tell the man had no weapon, but she could not be sure of this; or that the colonel was not also armed.

There were two police cars, which had been placed so as to form a chicane; it would have been possible to get past them but only with some difficulty and at low speed. If such an attempt had been made it was almost certain that the police would have opened fire; they were not noted for their restraint in the use of the weapons with which they were equipped; they were inclined to shoot first and ask

9

questions afterwards—or not to ask questions at all.

There were four men altogether, and one of them walked with a kind of arrogant swagger towards the black car. Rias had lowered the window on his side and the policeman came up to it and looked at him.

'What is the meaning of this?' Rias demanded. 'Why have we been stopped?'

'We are stopping all traffic,' the policeman said. 'It is according to orders.' He was young, long-jawed, with a black moustache. When he spoke his teeth gleamed whitely beneath it.

'Orders from whom?'

'That is not for me to say. I must ask you to identify yourselves.'

'My name is Rias—Colonel Rias. Possibly you have heard of me.'

It was evident that the man had; he reacted with a slight jerk of the head, and he peered even more closely at the colonel, who for his part did not offer any other evidence of identification beyond his spoken word.

'It is late to be travelling, Colonel.'

'There is no law forbidding me to travel at whatever hour I wish, day or night.' Rias spoke imperiously, as a man aware of addressing an inferior. The policeman was conscious of the difference in rank and it affected his confidence. Rias was not the easiest of men to outface. 'Now,' he said, 'perhaps you will allow us to proceed on our way.'

But the policeman, though he might have been somewhat overawed, stood his ground. 'And you are going where?'

'To my hacienda at Los Pinos.'

'That is fifty kilometres from here. A long way to travel in the middle of the night.'

'The distance is no concern of yours.'

The policeman glanced at the two passengers in the back of the car. Harrera's hat was pulled down over his eyes and it was difficult to see his face clearly. 'And who are these?'

'Friends of mine.'

'They also have names?'

'They have names but I see no necessity for you to know them. They are my guests who will be staying with me at the hacienda. Now will you permit us to be on our way?'

The policeman hesitated. 'I am not sure I can do that. Not until I have been in touch with my headquarters. I have had orders, you see.'

'What is your name?' Rias's voice was like ice.

'Perez.'

'And is it your desire, Señor Perez, to make a career for yourself in the police?'

'Yes, Colonel.'

'Then perhaps I may suggest to you that in delaying me and my guests in this completely unjustified manner you are hardly doing yourself any service in that respect. In fact, I

11

think I may go further and suggest that if you do not immediately stop this charade and allow us to continue our journey without further delay you might as well give up all hope of even wearing that uniform for more than another day. Do you get my meaning, Perez?'

Perez got the meaning; he would have had to be obtuse indeed not to have done so; it had been spelt out clearly enough and he must have had no doubt that Rias had the power to break him completely if that was his desire. He hesitated a moment or two longer, then suddenly turned and snarled an order at the other men. One of them got into one of the cars and moved it a little in order to widen the chicane.

'You may proceed, Colonel,' Perez said.

Rias nodded curtly and spoke to the driver. 'Move it, Sergeant.'

As soon as they were clear of the roadblock the sergeant accelerated quickly without waiting for instructions from Rias; he seemed to be well aware that there was now an even more urgent need for speed.

Rias turned in his seat and addressed Harrera. 'It seems we have been betrayed. Now it is touch and go.'

'You think the roadblock was there to intercept us?'

'I am sure of it.'

'Then why did the man let us through?'

'It is my belief that his orders had not been sufficiently precise; he had not been given any names. No doubt he had been told to stop any car trying to pass and to check with headquarters before letting it proceed. Fortunately I was able to scare him with that threat of putting a finish to his career. He probably sets a high value on his job. The irony of it is that by letting us slip through his fingers he has almost certainly made sure of losing it. He will be lucky if he does not end up in gaol or with a bullet in his head.'

'Poor man,' Margarita said. She could not help feeling pity for the young policeman. He had had a difficult choice to make and had picked the wrong alternative.

'What will he do now, do you think?' Harrera asked.

'Almost certainly he is already getting in touch with his superiors and telling them what has occurred. They will be stirred to activity when he gives them my name. It is a pity I had to tell him who I was, but there was no alternative if I wished to intimidate him. Now it will not be long before those two cars we left blocking the road come after us in hot pursuit. Others too, perhaps. With luck they will go to Los Pinos, but it would be unwise to count on that.'

Margarita was silent. Her worst fears had been realised. Things had begun to go wrong.

CHAPTER TWO

ENCOUNTER

There was very little traffic on the road; they had overtaken two or three lorries and had met a few travelling in the opposite direction, but there had been no other cars. It was getting on for 2 a.m. when they came to a fork in the road. With scarcely any slackening of speed the sergeant took the big car on to the right-hand highway and from that point the surface deteriorated to such an extent that the springs of the car came under continual stress and the passengers were subjected to some discomfort.

Harrera glanced back through the rear window and Margarita followed his example. There was no sign of any pursuit; the headlamps of a car behind them would have been instantly visible, but there were none. And soon the fork had been left far behind and the black car still plunged on into the night.

'I think it is going to be all right,' Margarita said. It was more of a hope than an honest belief, and she spoke with the intention of giving perhaps some encouragement to the man sitting beside her.

Harrera ignored the remark, but Rias

turned and said with a certain acidity: 'Take nothing for granted. We are not out of the wood yet. Someone has certainly betrayed us and it is a question just how much information has been passed on. There may already be a reception committee waiting at the airfield.'

'And if there is?'

'Then we shall have to do what is necessary.'

He did not elaborate, and again the girl prayed that there would be no violence. But she knew that it might well be a vain prayer: Rias was a man who would not hesitate to employ ruthless methods to achieve his objective. But in the present situation would such methods prove effective? Suppose the odds against him were too great. He and the sergeant could not fight an army. She feared the operation might end in disaster, but there was nothing that she could do to prevent it; events must now take their course.

She heard Rias say to the driver: 'Stop the car here, Sergeant.'

On the right was a wire fence running parallel to the road, and a short distance further on was a gateway. The gate was standing open and to the left of it inside the fence was a small wooden building like an army hut. There was no light showing anywhere and no sign of life.

'I think perhaps we are fortunate,' Rias said. 'But it will be best to make sure.'

He got out of the car and walked towards

15

the gateway. He went inside the fence and disappeared from sight. The others waited in the car, saying nothing. Rias seemed to be gone a long time, but in fact it was only a few minutes; then he came back running. He got into the car, panting a little.

'All is well. There is no one about. Get moving, Sergeant.'

The girl began to breathe more easily, though she still felt on edge; the operation could well have reached the critical stage.

The sergeant steered the car in through the gateway, and a moment or two later there was turf under the wheels. The aircraft was revealed suddenly in the beam of the headlamps; it was a light twin-engine monoplane, silver-grey in colour, and it was taxying into position. As they approached it turned and came to a halt, ready for the take-off.

'Good,' Rias said. 'Everything seems to be according to plan.'

The engines of the plane were ticking over when the black car stopped a few yards away from it. The four occupants got out, and the sergeant opened the boot and began taking out the luggage that was in it. The others helped to transfer the suitcases to the plane while the pilot remained in his seat ready to get the aircraft away as soon as everyone was on board.

Rias shouted to him: 'Is all in order? Any

problems?'

'No problems,' the pilot answered. 'All set to go as soon as you give the signal.'

For people who were leaving their country perhaps for ever there was not a great deal of luggage. They were in the act of loading the last two suitcases when their activities were rudely interrupted by the arrival of a second car. They had been so preoccupied with what they were doing that none of them noticed it until they were caught in the glare of its headlamps. They swung round then, dazzled by that brilliant white light which revealed only too clearly the silver-grey plane, the would-be passengers and the black car that had brought them.

For a moment nobody moved. The second car came to a halt some twenty paces away, and a man shouted:

'Stay where you are. Put your hands up.'

Dazzled as they were, they could only dimly observe that the doors of the other car had been thrown open and that men were getting out. There appeared to be four of them and there could be little doubt that all were armed.

Without warning Rias began shooting. From somewhere on his person he had fished out a big automatic pistol; he fired a couple of shots and dived for shelter behind the black car. The sergeant had been standing close to the open door of the car on the driver's side, and without waiting for orders he ducked inside and came out with a submachine-gun. He poked it over the top of the bonnet and fired one short burst and then another.

The men who had come out of the other car were not slow in answering the fire, and it was no time to be standing around and waiting to be hit. Yet Harrera had still not moved; it was as though his brain had been paralysed by this rapid turn of events and refused to give any orders to his limbs. It was the girl who reacted to the danger. She shouted to him to get down, and when he still did not move she seized his arm and tried to drag him to the ground by sheer force.

It seemed to bring him to his senses; he gave a start and went down on his knees and then flat on the ground. The two of them lay with the black car shielding them from the men who were firing from the other side while Rias and the sergeant kept them at bay.

Rias turned his head and shouted: 'Get into the plane. Tell him to take off. We'll deal with things here.'

'No,' Harrera said. 'No, I will not do that.'

It would have been a risky thing to do anyway; if he stood up to climb into the plane he would present a clear target for the men with the guns.

Rias said no more; he had emptied his pistol and was replacing the empty clip with a full one from his pocket. The sergeant crawled round to the front of the car, rested his elbows on the ground and fired a burst which doused the headlamps of the other car.

Two of the attackers began running towards the black car. Rias stood up and fired his automatic, which made a hard staccato sound as the bullets slammed out of the barrel. One of the men gave a scream. He fell forward on to his face, his gun slipping from his hand, and did not get up. The other man was almost at the car when the sergeant shot him with the submachine-gun and tore a large part of his head away.

Rias shouted again at Harrera: 'Now! Go now, I beg you. Don't be so damned stubborn. Go!'

He was still standing. In his eagerness to persuade Harrera to get into the plane he was ignoring the risk to himself. It was true that he was no longer in the harsh glare of the smashed headlamps, but he was not invisible. He began to speak again, but the words seemed to catch in his throat. He clutched at the roof of the black car for support, but his hand slid off it; his legs bent at the knees and he went down. He made an effort to get up but could not do it. He gave a kind of sigh as though it were the last breath going out of his body, and collapsed.

Harrera got up and ran to him, crouching low. He lifted Rias's head. 'Marcos,' he said. It was scarcely more than a whisper. 'Marcos, old friend, do not leave me.'

Rias did not answer, did not move.

Margarita kneeled at the other side of Rias. She took his wrist in her hand and felt for the pulse. There was nothing.

'He is dead, Papa.'

There was another burst of firing from the men on the far side of the black car. A bullet shattered one of the windows, another ricochetted off the metal, whining thinly. The sergeant fitted a new magazine to his submachine-gun, slipped round the tail of the car and started running towards the other men, firing from the hip.

One of the men took a blast in the stomach and fell to the ground screaming. The other man was taking cover behind one of the open doors. He rested his gun on the window frame and fired through the opening. His first shot hit the sergeant in the chest, and he stumbled and fell. The man ran to him and pressed the muzzle of his revolver to the sergeant's head and fired again.

Margarita tugged at her father's sleeve. 'We must go. We must go now.'

Harrera got to his feet and with the girl still pulling at his arm stumbled like a blind man towards the door of the plane. He was climbing in when the man with the revolver came round the front of the black car and began firing. A bullet ripped into the fuselage three inches from Harrera's hand. The man crouched, steadied the revolver with both hands, took careful aim and pressed the trigger. There was a faint click as the hammer fell on a dead cartridge.

Margarita could hear the man cursing. He tipped the dead shells out of the cylinder and fumbled in his pocket for more live rounds. Harrera was slow in getting into the plane and the girl urged him to hurry; there was so little time. She glanced at the man with the revolver; he was pushing a round into the cylinder. The distance between him and the girl was no more than a dozen paces and she could see that he had receding hair and a straggling moustache. He lifted his head and looked at her, and for a moment their eyes met. She saw the white of his teeth as he grinned with a kind of wild beast ferocity. Then he flicked the cylinder back into place and took aim again.

She saw the barrel of the revolver pointing at her and she could not move; she could do nothing but stand rigidly, waiting for the man to press the trigger. He would kill her and then he would run to the plane, climb inside and kill her father; there was no way of stopping him. She thought of pleading with him, begging him not to shoot. But she spoke no word; it would have been useless; he was not in the business of sparing lives. She could see his finger on the trigger and could almost sense the pressure of it that would set off the mechanism. She closed her eyes, waiting for the shot.

The sound of the gun was surprisingly loud; it was as though it had been fired practically in her ear. Yet she felt no impact of the bullet. It was hardly believable; at that range how could he have failed to hit his target?

She opened her eyes and saw the man lying on the ground, his right arm stretched out in front of him and the hand still grasping the revolver. She could not understand it. Was it an hallucination? Could it really be the man who had been about to shoot her lying there on the ground?

She swayed slightly; she had a sensation of giddiness and there was a weakness in her legs. But then she felt a hand grip her right arm, supporting her, and she heard a man's voice close to her ear.

'You'd better climb in now,' the man said. 'I'm going to take her up.'

She turned her head and saw the pilot leaning out of the doorway of the plane. He had his left hand on her arm and in the other hand was a pistol. She realised then why the report of the gun had sounded so loud; it had been he who had fired, aiming past her at the man with the revolver.

'Hurry!' he said. 'There's no time to waste.' He was a tall young man with a mass of curly hair and a sun-tanned face. She had forgotten his existence in the stress of the brief engagement; she supposed he had been keeping his head down until the crucial

22

moment when he had taken a decisive hand in the game.

She felt she ought to thank him, for he had undoubtedly saved her life; but it was hardly the time for courtesies, and she said nothing.

'Hurry!' he said again. 'I think we've got more trouble on our hands if we don't get out of here good and fast.'

She was not sure what he meant by that, but she climbed into the plane and he closed the door. Harrera was sitting in one of the seats and looking ill. The pilot went quickly to the controls, and the engines made a racket as he got ready to take off.

Margarita glanced out through one of the windows and saw what he had meant by more trouble; away in the distance by the entrance to the airfield lights were showing and it was evident that reinforcements had arrived to back up the four men who had been shot. A moment later she saw that two cars were heading towards the plane, their headlamps glaring.

Harrera said fussily: 'What are you doing? What are you looking at out there?'

'There are two cars coming this way.'

'Ah!' Harrera said; but he made no move to look through the window himself. He seemed resigned to letting events take their course; there was after all nothing useful that he could do. The information that there might now be more pursuers to reckon with appeared to leave him unmoved.

The engines had revved up and the plane was starting its take-off run. Margarita estimated that the leading car was about two hundred metres away. The plane gathered speed, bumping a little. She saw the cars alter direction, the evident intention of the drivers being to cut across the line of take-off. Aircraft and vehicles converged with frightening rapidity. Would they, she wondered, collide before the plane could become airborne? She tensed, anticipating the shock of impact.

There came a sudden chatter of small-arms fire. Two men were leaning out of the cars and firing at the plane; but it was no easy task to hit a moving target from a moving platform and the shots were flying wide. Yet if the cars came close enough it might be a different story, for the target would then loom very large indeed.

It seemed to Margarita that the drivers had judged distance and direction with surprising accuracy; one of them at least appeared certain to be on the take-off line before the plane reached the spot. She wondered what the pilot would do. Would he try to stop the plane or change its direction? Would there in fact be time to do anything? And the men in the cars—would they jump out and run for safety or were they prepared to risk their lives in order to prevent President Harrera from escaping? The thoughts flashed through her mind as she waited for the seemingly inevitable collision.

But then she felt the nose of the aircraft lift, and a moment later it was airborne. But would it gain height quickly enough to clear the cars or would the undercarriage touch the nearer of them and cause the plane to crash? She felt her body forced hard against the back of the seat as the plane climbed, and she knew that it had cleared the obstacle and nothing would stop it now. She felt a sense of overwhelming relief, and she was turning to speak to her father when some bullets ripped through the floor of the cabin and she heard him utter a cry of pain.

She went to him and saw blood flowing from his cheek, and she was appalled by the thought that at this last moment he might have been seriously injured or even mortally wounded. But in answer to her anxious question he told her testily that it was nothing, the merest scratch. He seemed ashamed at having cried out, and in fact it was, as he had said, no more than a scratch. It had not even been inflicted by a bullet except in a secondary manner, but by a flying splinter of wood.

And after that there were no more alarms. The plane flew northward at a low altitude in order to creep under any radar detection, and within an hour it had crossed the border.

Rias was dead; the sergeant was dead; four nameless other men were dead; but Harrera

25

was alive and a free man. And that after all had been the object of the exercise.

CHAPTER THREE

MEAT AND DRINK

The man's name was Pedro Mendes, but he was generally known in the circle in which he plied his trade as The Weasel. He was a small, soft-footed, light-fingered, quick-moving man, who could worm and wriggle his way into places that were inaccessible to any ordinary person. And this was a great advantage in his particular occupation, which was a certain kind of professional photography.

Mendes was a free-lance who specialised in pictures of the candid or revelatory variety. He liked to photograph people when they were off guard or caught in embarrassing situations. He made much use of the telescopic lens and the concealed camera, and he sold his work to the kind of magazine or newspaper that was in the business of publishing the type of picture that he had for sale.

Some people called it the Gutter Press, but if there was money to be had in the gutter Pedro Mendes was not above stooping to pick it up. Yet oddly enough some of his most profitable work was never put before the eye of the general public, for very often it was possible to command a higher price by going to the people whose images were in the photographs and who had a strange but powerful aversion to the idea of such images being available for any Tom, Dick or Harry to gaze at and drool over.

This curious obsession with privacy amused Mendes, because these people were often the very same characters who courted publicity in the ordinary way and never seemed able to get too much of it. But of course there was publicity and there was publicity, and Mendes was very glad there was, because it certainly made life a great deal richer and jollier for men like him.

Though it was largely his activities that had earned him the name of Weasel, he had also a certain physical resemblance to that rapacious little carnivore. His features were thin and pinched, and he had bright, inquiring eyes that missed nothing. He had a receding forehead, small ears and very little chin to speak of. His voice was high-pitched and squeaky, and when he was excited he stuttered slightly.

His origins were somewhat obscure, but it was believed that he came from somewhere in Central America, though he was certainly not Mexican. He travelled widely and was reputed to speak a dozen languages with reasonable fluency. He gambled in most of the places where people went to gamble and had been known to win as much as a quarter of a million dollars in one evening in Las Vegas; or so it was said. No one could remember his losing money on the gaming-tables, but perhaps memories were poor on that point; people remembered what they wished to remember and forgot what they wished to forget, and the idea that The Weasel ever had a losing streak would not have fitted the accepted view of him.

Some maintained that he had sold his soul to the devil and that was why he had the devil's own luck, and they could hardly wait for Beelzebub to come and claim his own when the time ran out; they just hoped they would be around to see it. Some of those who had had their photographs taken by him were the most eager of all to see him get his come-uppance, but he was a fly customer and very good at looking after Pedro Mendes.

It was in a place called St Martin in the Bahamas that Mendes took the photographs which almost cost him his life. He was there for the gambling, which was the chief industry in St Martin, but as usual he had his photographic equipment with him and was keeping his eye open for a likely subject for the lens. And then one day, as he was strolling down the principal shopping street of St Martin, enjoying the sunshine and the general air of prosperity that seemed to be all around him, he caught sight of Señora Roberta

Zaragoza coming out of a jeweller's shop with a small parcel dangling from her hand. There was a yellow taxicab waiting by the kerb and she got into it and was carried away. Mendes was so surprised that he almost omitted to take the number of the cab.

He was quite sure that the woman was Señora Zaragoza. The señora was the wife of General Mateo Zaragoza, who was a very prominent man in the country in which Mendes had been born. There had been much publicity when he married Roberta Lopez; which was only to be expected, seeing that Roberta was a noted beauty and less than half the age of the general.

It was said that he was quite besotted with her and showered her with expensive presents and followed her round like a dog for months before she finally consented to marry him. Many people were astonished that she should ever have done so; for the general, besides being so much older than the lady, could hardly have been described as handsome. He was rather short, rather stout, and had a heavy saturnine face and only a sprinkling of greasy hair on his head. He did, however, possess considerable wealth and had much influence in the country. He was, moreover, a man of violent temper and one whom it was inadvisable to antagonise; he was inclined to deal harshly and ruthlessly with those who were so unfortunate or reckless as to arouse his animosity.

Mendes wondered what Roberta could be doing in the Bahamas. He wondered also whether the general was with her. Somehow, he could not imagine Zaragoza taking much delight in the frivolous activities and pleasures of this island in the sun. But perhaps Roberta had persuaded him to come.

Mendes was sufficiently curious to make a telephone call to a contact in his native country, from which he had been absent for a considerable length of time. The contact's name was Garcia and he worked on a daily paper called *La Prensa.* Thus he could be relied upon to be up to date with just about everything that was going on.

Garcia was not a personal friend of Mendes; he was merely a business acquaintance. Mendes had similar contacts in other countries; he paid each a modest retainer and extra fees if they came up with anything useful. Through them he was able to keep in touch with the comings and goings of people in the public eye, and this was very necessary in his line of work.

His first question to Garcia concerned the whereabouts of General Zaragoza.

'Is he out of the country?'

Garcia said that this was certainly not so. He himself had actually seen the general in person the previous day at a military ceremony.

30

'Why do you ask?'

'Never mind,' Mendes said. 'Was Señora Zaragoza with him?'

'Why, no,' Garcia said. 'The lovely Roberta is taking a trip to Europe. The last I heard she was in Paris staying with a cousin who married a French artist named Dubois.'

'Is that a fact?'

'You have my word. What is all this about?'

'Nothing. Just checking up.'

'You never check up without a purpose. Are you on to something?'

'Nothing that would interest you.'

Garcia laughed. 'I don't believe it. I can tell when you've got your nose into the dirt. But a word of warning—if it's anything to do with General Zaragoza, watch your step. He can be poison.'

'You don't have to tell me,' Mendes said.

He wondered whether to drop the matter there. What Garcia had said was true; Zaragoza was poison. Besides, would there be any money in it? And if there was money, would it be enough to warrant the undoubted risk? Perhaps it would be best to forget it and not waste his time. Maybe the woman he had seen had not been Roberta Zaragoza, just somebody who looked like the señora. But he knew that it had been her; in his own mind he had no doubt at all; he had been too close to her to make any mistake. And the señora was supposed to be in Paris. So why was she here?

And did Zaragoza know or was the cousin, Madame Dubois, covering up for her?

Mendes had to know the answers. It might be dangerous, it might be unprofitable, but he could not let it go. It was a challenge to his professionalism and he had to accept the challenge.

It was not difficult to trace the driver of the taxicab, a young black with large hands and a very human weakness for money. A generous transfer of paper from Mendes's wallet to one of the large black hands was sufficient to stir the man's memory. He had not forgotten the lady he had picked up at the jeweller's shop; she was not the kind a man would forget easily. The cab-driver grinned widely.

'Very beautiful. And the figure! Man!'

'You had seen her before, perhaps?'

'No, never.'

'You know her name?'

'No, she don't tell me her name. No call to.'

'Where did you take her?'

'Don't rightly recall. My memory that bad, you wouldn't b'lieve.'

Mendes did not believe. He made another transfer of paper from the wallet to the receptive hand. 'Will that make it better?'

Miraculously, the memory improved; the address was lodged in one of the recesses of the cab-driver's brain and the money eased it out. Mendes made a note of it and thanked the driver for his assistance.

'Any time, man, any time.'

*　　*　　*

Mendes drove out to the place in his rented car. It was five miles out of town, a luxury bungalow standing in spacious grounds where a lot of landscaping had been done with rocks and running water and the like. There were various kinds of tropical trees and shrubs, and the bungalow itself was on two levels and had a red roof and a verandah and rough stone walls.

Mendes drove past the entrance for about a hundred yards and parked his car at the side of the road. He walked back and went in through a gateway where a pair of iron gates hung on brick pillars were standing open. A shingle drive led up to the bungalow, and he went to the front door and rang the bell and waited. After a moment or two the door was opened by a young black girl who was evidently a servant. Mendes thought she looked at him with some suspicion.

'Yes?' she said.

'I wonder whether I have come to the right house,' Mendes said. 'This is where Mr Brown lives, isn't it?'

'Mr Brown?'

'Yes; Mr Roger Brown.'

'No, sir; I never heard of no Mr Roger Brown. This here place belong to Mr Hutchinson. He's away right now but there's a

33

friend of his staying here for the present. Mr Johnson. Him and his wife.'

'I see,' Mendes said. 'I must have been misinformed. So you don't know where I could find Mr Brown?'

'No, sir. Like I said, I ain't never heard of him.'

Mendes thanked her and walked away, thinking. He wondered whether the cab-driver had fed him with the wrong address, taking his money and laughing at him as soon as his back was turned. But he doubted it; there would have been no bonus in it for him. So who was Mr Johnson?

He came to the entrance gate, stepped into the road and began walking back to where he had left his car. He had covered about half the distance when another car came up from that direction and went past. It was a white BMW convertible with the hood down and he saw it turn in at the gateway from which he had just come.

'So,' he muttered softly, 'that is our Mr Johnson. How very interesting. How very remarkable.'

He had recognised the man at the wheel of the BMW, and if he was for the present calling himself Mr Johnson that could only be because he had no wish to advertise his true identity. But Mendes knew him by sight as well as he knew Roberta Zaragoza, and the name he knew him by was Alvarez—General Bernardo

Alvarez.

Alvarez was close on forty years old, but he looked little more than thirty. He was ten years younger than Zaragoza and he was lithe and athletic and handsome. He also ranked higher in the army list than the older man. Whether or not all this irked Zaragoza it was impossible to say; he gave no sign that it did, and the two high-ranking officers were close friends; at least to all outward appearances. Together they represented a power in the land that was second to none. It was said that even President Harrera stood somewhat in awe of them and did his best not to antagonise this influential pair.

But how long, Mendes wondered, would this grand partnership endure if Zaragoza were to discover that his comrade-in-arms was sharing a luxury bungalow in the Bahamas with the adorable woman who had first bewitched and then consented to marry him? Mendes knew the answer to that question: it would not endure a moment longer; there would be an explosion of shattering intensity, and either Alvarez or Zaragoza himself would die.

Mendes was amazed at the risk Alvarez and Roberta were prepared to take. And then he recalled a rumour he had heard that there had once been something going between the two before the marriage of the lady to Zaragoza. He had dismissed it at the time as mere scandal, but maybe there had been truth in it. So why had she accepted Zaragoza? Had she temporarily fallen out with Alvarez and succumbed to Zaragoza's importuning in a moment of pique? Or had it been a question of money? It was no secret that Zaragoza was far richer than Alvarez, and Roberta probably liked the good things in life that great wealth could bring. Anyway, the reason was of no importance; it was the fact that mattered, and the undoubted fact was that Zaragoza's wife was having an affair with Alvarez.

So what was there in this curious business for Pedro Mendes?

Again he had an impulse to drop the matter, because there were limits to the risks even he would take in the pursuit of his calling, and the risks here had every indication of being very great indeed. Nevertheless, he was still reluctant to let it go; more so now perhaps than before. He knew that, come what might, he had to go through with it.

He did some reconnoitring and discovered that a narrow lane divided the grounds of the bungalow from the property on one side of it. The lane branched off at right angles to the road where Mendes had parked his car; it was unmetalled and it was closed in by trees and other growth which made a high wall on either side and the branches of which met and mingled overhead so that it was like walking through a green tunnel.

Mendes was unable to see the bungalow because of this thick growth, but he could make a pretty good guess as to where it was in relation to his own position, and when he had walked about fifty yards down the lane he decided to make an attempt to get round to the rear of the building where there would almost certainly be a garden.

He pushed his way into the undergrowth and reflected that a machete would have been useful because it really was rather like going into a jungle. And then he came up against an even more difficult obstacle, for about ten yards in from the fringe of the trees was a fence of vertical wooden boards about eight feet high, and the tops of the boards were cut into sharp points to make it all the harder for an intruder to climb over them. It was evident that Mr Hutchinson, the owner of the property, liked to safeguard his privacy; and that probably went for Mr Johnson too while he was in residence.

Mendes went along the fence looking for a gap or a loose board where he could squeeze his way through, but the woodwork was all in good condition and nowhere could he find a weakness in the defences. He could have climbed over without much difficulty if it had not been for the spikes, but these deterred him, offering as they did no comfortable hold for the fingers. He noticed, however, that some of the larger trees growing close to the fence had spread their branches beyond it, and he was soon able to find one that he could climb. As luck would have it there was a stout bough in a convenient position and he found little difficulty in crawling along it and dropping to the soft ground on the other side of the fence.

He was now inside the garden, and as he moved cautiously forward the cover became less dense, giving way to ornamental shrubs and bushes and small trees, with beds of flowers here and there and paths meandering between them. Suddenly he caught sight of the bungalow; it was on his right and about thirty yards away. There was a terrace with a lot of garden furniture such as tables with parasols and lounging-chairs and hammocks and a teak bench or two; and there were small palms and exotic plants in tubs, and vines climbing up trellis; all of which looked very pleasant in the warm sunlight.

But what made it even more pleasant to the eye of Pedro Mendes was a swimming-pool below the terrace and lying on a sunbed close beside it Señora Roberta Zaragoza, soaking up the ultraviolet rays and wearing nothing but a pair of dark glasses with huge white frames.

Mendes was hidden from sight behind a clump of bamboo, but he was at a higher level than the swimming-pool, and by parting the canes he was able to get an excellent view. And he had not been there more than half a minute when he saw General Alvarez walk out on to the terrace and descend to the edge of the pool where the señora was lying. Alvarez was wearing a crimson bathrobe, but when he got to the pool he shrugged it off and revealed that underneath it he was as naked as the lady.

Mendes cursed softly. Here was the kind of subject that was meat and drink to him and he had no camera; he had left it in the car. Well, he would just have to go and fetch it, hoping that no one would go away during his absence. He might have asked them to stick around for a while, but he doubted whether that would have been a good idea; they might have received the suggestion with some lack of grace.

Taking care to make no sound that might alarm the couple, he left the bamboo clump and made his way stealthily back to the fence. It was easy enough to climb on the inner side because of the horizontal timbers to which the boards were nailed, and with the help of the overhanging bough he was able to negotiate the spikes without trouble.

Once back in the lane he started running, and he made it to the car in double-quick time, meeting no one on the way. He unlocked the car, picked up the camera-case and slung it over his shoulder by the carrying strap in order to leave his hands free for climbing the fence.

Then he ran back to the lane.

CHAPTER FOUR

IN FOCUS

He was dripping with sweat when he reached the bamboo clump, and his fingers were so slippery that he had some difficulty in making the necessary adjustments to the camera. He could hear the sound of voices coming from the other side of the bamboo and knew therefore that the man and the woman had not gone away; but when he parted the canes he was disgusted to find that he could not see them. The sunbed was still there but no one was lying on it, and though Alvarez's bathrobe was hanging on the chair where he had dropped it the man himself was nowhere to be seen.

The voices were silent for the moment, but then they broke out again. There was some laughter and the sound of splashing water, and Mendes, switching his gaze to the left, saw that Alvarez and Roberta were in the pool and having quite a time of it. Just like a pair of kids, Mendes thought; but without condemnation. Let them have their fun; he was a broad-minded man and had no objection.

He made a few more adjustments to the camera and took some shots of the frolicking in the water. Later, when the bathers climbed out of the pool, he was able to get some more pictures, the two well-shaped bodies dripping water and the droplets glittering in the sunlight; all most artistic. He felt a sense of joy, of deep satisfaction with a task being well performed; and this was quite independent of any possible value that might be put on the results.

So absorbed had he become in what he was doing that he was oblivious of the danger inherent in his situation. It was a faint sound behind him which brought him back to an awareness of that danger. He turned his head and saw a tall black man in faded jeans looking down at him.

'What in hell you think you doin' there?' the man demanded.

Mendes stowed the camera in its case and got up quickly. The man was probably a gardener; he was carrying a machete in his right hand and Mendes hoped it was simply for cutting weeds; it looked highly lethal. He did not answer the question because there was no answer he could give that would satisfactorily explain his presence behind the bamboo clump.

He heard Alvarez's voice. 'What's going on up there?'

The black shouted: 'We got a Paul Pry here, Mis' Johnson. He got a camera.'

Alvarez swore explosively. 'Hold him, Josh.

41

Don't let the swine getaway. I'll be right there.'

Mendes took a tentative step. Josh waggled the machete. 'Don' try it, man. I could slice you up real good.'

Mendes did not doubt it. The black scared him; he looked capable of any amount of mayhem. But he was even more scared of Alvarez, who was really just as bad as Zaragoza in the poison line; so he made a sudden dart to the left and was on his way before the black could lift the machete for a cut at him.

He had a few yards start and he was up on the bough of the tree by the time his pursuer got to the fence. The man slashed at him with the machete, but the blade hit one of the smaller branches an inch or two away from Mendes's right leg and became imbedded in the wood. While the black was struggling to free it Mendes took the opportunity to drop to the ground.

Unfortunately for him, he twisted his ankle in the process and a cry of pain was forced from his lips. A moment later he saw the black head of the man called Josh appear over the top of the fence and he knew that, twisted ankle or no twisted ankle, he had to be on his way. And then another head appeared above the boards, that of Bernardo Alvarez. The general was once again in the crimson bathrobe, but what was of greater significance was the fact that he had a revolver in his right hand.

Mendes was amazed. What kind of man was it who carried a revolver even in the pocket of his bathrobe? The answer to that of course was a man like General Bernardo Alvarez, who was so used to living in a country where he was under constant threat of attack that self-protection became second nature to him. Which was just too bad for Pedro Mendes.

'Stop exactly where you are,' Alvarez said. 'Make one false move and I'll kill you.'

Mendes did not believe everything he heard, but he believed that. Alvarez spoke with utter conviction, and there was a cold anger in him that frightened Mendes more than any wild outburst of rage would have done.

'You rat,' Alvarez said. 'You damned mean little rat.'

Mendes had the crazy thought of correcting him, of telling him that he had got the wrong animal and that the word he should have used was weasel. But he said nothing.

Alvarez spoke to the black. 'Get him. Bring him back here.'

The black had stopped to see what Alvarez would do; now he began to climb over the fence. Mendes decided that it was better to take the risk of going than the greater risk of staying. He turned and ran.

The bullet went past his ear like someone whispering a secret and imbedded itself in the trunk of a tree. It set the adrenalin flowing faster, and two more shots kept up the good work, though neither of them was as close as the first. He came out into the lane with his twisted ankle threatening to chuck in the sponge at any moment and bring him to his knees. But he gritted his teeth and pounded on.

He was thirty yards up the lane when he glanced back and saw the black come into sight. He yelled at Mendes to stop and waved the machete threateningly, which was hardly the most alluring of invitations and had no effect whatever in slackening the pace of Mendes's retreat. He came to the road and saw the car ahead waiting for him like a haven of safety, and he put on a final spurt and reached it before the black came round the corner.

He already had the key in his hand, and he stabbed it into the lock and tried to turn it; but it refused to budge. He glanced back along the road and saw the black suddenly appear and come loping towards him with an odd high-stepping action, as though his legs had been the connecting-rods of a donkey-engine.

Mendes turned his attention again to the key and discovered that he had not pushed it completely in. When he had done so it turned easily enough. He opened the door, threw the camera in its case on to the passenger seat and got in faster than he could remember ever having got into a car before. There was nothing like the threat of a couple of feet of wide steel blade to lend speed to one's actions.

The black arrived just as he was pulling the door shut, and he aimed a swipe with the machete which would surely have decapitated Mendes if he had had his head out of the car. The blade hit the door and it must have jarred the black's hand, but he gave no sign that it had. Mendes finished shutting the door and the black tried to wrench it open; but it was locked and the glass was up.

The frustration seemed to throw him into a complete frenzy and he started lashing at the roof of the car as if to chop his way in. Mendes hoped the roof was strong enough to resist the attack, because the last thing he wanted was the machete blade coming through and slicing into his head. He reflected that the hire company was not going to be very pleased about it when he took the car back, but that was the least of his worries. He failed to see what the black had to be so upset about; he had not even had his photograph taken. So maybe that was what was biting him; maybe he thought it was racial discrimination and resented it.

He had the key in the ignition and the starter whirred and nothing happened. It was a hell of a time for the engine to play hard to get. But he gave it a few more tries and suddenly the machinery came to life and it was

45

such a relief he almost shouted for joy. And then he looked in the mirror and saw Alvarez coming up the road, bathrobe flapping and revolver waving.

Alvarez's feet were bare and his hair was all over the place after his frolics in the water, and it would have been funny if it had not been so serious. Mendes felt no inclination to laughter; he just wanted to get away. He put the car into gear and got it moving, the black running alongside and taking more swipes with the machete as long as he could keep up.

Mendes glanced again into the mirror and saw Alvarez take up a gunslinger's stance and aim at the receding car. A bullet shattered the rear window, and Mendes felt his skin crawl. And then he came to a bend in the road and knew he had made it, because even if Alvarez went back and fetched out the BMW he was never going to catch the rented car now. And thank God Alvarez did not know him by sight, otherwise he would really have been in the stew; he would have been in it up to his ears.

*   *   *

Mendes put another call through to Garcia later that day and asked his journalist contact whether he knew anything regarding the movements of General Bernardo Alvarez. He was pretty certain that the man who had shot at him was Alvarez, but he wanted to be dead

46

sure.

'He's on leave,' Garcia said. 'I understand he's out of the country but nobody seems to know where he's gone.'

'I think I could tell you,' Mendes said. 'But I'm not going to.'

He could hear Garcia sucking his breath in past his teeth. 'Don't tell me you're getting involved with him now. That would really be taking a risk. He can be worse than Zaragoza.'

'I know he can.'

'You should take care of yourself,' Garcia said. He was maybe thinking about his retainer and the other payments.

'I'll do that,' Mendes said. 'Don't worry.' And he rang off.

*   *   *

The man at the rental garage was indeed none too pleased when Mendes took the car back. He wanted to know what had happened to it.

'I was involved in a slight accident,' Mendes said.

'You mean somebody shot at you by accident? That's a bullet-hole, isn't it?'

'Well, yes,' Mendes admitted. 'But it was a mistake.'

'Mistakes like that could cost you your life.'

'I know,' Mendes said.

'And what are those marks on the roof? Looks like a bear's been crawling over it.'

'A man tried to cut it open with a machete.'

'Why?'

'He didn't tell me why and I didn't like to ask. He seemed bothered about something.'

'You'll have to pay for the damage, you know. It's not covered by the insurance.'

Mendes did not argue; he had no wish to make a fuss about it. The man looked happier when he handed over the dollars.

'You want another car?'

'Not today,' Mendes said. 'I'm leaving.'

He had decided that for the sake of his health it might be best to get away from the Bahamas without delay. It was not likely that Alvarez would succeed in tracking him down, but there was no sense in taking a chance on it. After all, he himself had encountered Roberta Zaragoza quite by accident, and accidents like that could happen again. He would hop on a plane to Miami and take it from there. Maybe another visit to Las Vegas would not be out of order.

*　　　*　　　*

Mendes gave a deal of thought to the question of whether or not to try to find a customer for the photographs. They had come out beautifully; he had never done a better piece of work and it seemed a pity not to market the product; a regrettable waste of time and effort. Yet always he came to the same conclusion: it was not safe to do so.

Besides, would a magazine or a newspaper take them? There might be some that would, but it was doubtful whether they would offer the kind of sum that would make it worth while to sell. It was not as though General Alvarez and General Zaragoza were figures of world-wide fame, influential though they might be in their own small country. The periodicals which might be most interested in them were those published in that country, and not one of them would have touched the pictures with a barge-pole; they would not have dared; or at least their publishers and editors would not. So the market was limited.

And always he came back to the risk to himself; for what editor would bother to keep the origin of the pictures a secret when Alvarez was asking questions? Especially if Alvarez was prepared to pay for the information. Mendes had no desire to spend the rest of his life running away from the general or his agents, and maybe not running fast enough when it came to the crunch.

The most likely buyer of course was Alvarez himself. He would certainly have been prepared to pay handsomely rather than let the photographs fall into the hands of General Zaragoza, the jealous and violent husband of the lady involved. But though Mendes might have obtained money from Alvarez, he doubted whether he would have enjoyed the

49

use of it for long. And on the whole he thought it was better not to have the money and live than have the money and end up on a mortuary slab.

So the pictures remained in his possession, unseen by any eyes but his own; and time passed and it looked as though they might remain for ever unsold. But then an event occurred in Central America, and Mendes believed he had a buyer.

CHAPTER FIVE

PRIVATE AND CONFIDENTIAL

'It was good of you to agree to see me, Mr Harris,' Mendes said. 'I think I can honestly assure you that you will not regret it.'

Mr Harris seemed to be rather less certain on that point. He looked at Mendes with some distaste, as though not particularly liking what he saw. Mendes himself was aware of not looking quite at his best; he was wearing a false beard and moustache and a blond wig and tinted glasses. He wondered whether the other man could see that the beard and wig were stage props. Perhaps so, but it did not matter; they were simply a precautionary measure, like the name of Smith which he had given to the woman who had answered the door.

Almost a year had passed since Mendes had come to the conclusion that he had a buyer for the photographs of Alvarez and Roberta. It had not been convenient for him to visit London during that period, besides which he had had some difficulty in locating his man. But he was here now and he was hopeful of striking a useful bargain.

Harris made a vague gesture towards a chair, and Mendes sat down. It was, he thought, a pleasant kind of room, a cross between a sitting-room and a library: one wall was lined with bookshelves, and under the window which looked out on to a well-kept lawn was a writing-table cluttered with papers.

'You had better tell me what it is you wished to see me about,' Harris said. 'My time—' He seemed to be about to say that his time was valuable but left the sentence incomplete, deciding perhaps that it would not have been altogether truthful to make such a claim. He was a lean middle-aged man, and he looked tired, not so much physically perhaps as mentally; there were pouches under his eyes and there was a kind of ashen quality about the skin of his face, the bony structure of the skull clearly discernible beneath it. He was dressed in a sober grey suit which was well cut, and there was a certain air of distinction about him of which Mendes was immediately aware.

'I have something to sell,' Mendes said. He

51

was carrying a leather briefcase, and he gave it a little pat with his hand as he spoke to indicate that his wares were inside it.

A frown of irritation appeared on Mr Harris's face. 'A door-to-door salesman! If you think I am interested in an encyclopedia or double-glazing you are wasting your time and mine.'

Mendes gave an emphatic shake of the head. 'Oh, no, it is nothing like that. I am not a door-to-door salesman as you suggest. Yours is the only door I have come to because you are the one person I believe will buy what I have to sell. You are interested now?'

He could see that he had caught the interest of the man in the grey suit; there was curiosity in Harris's eyes. Mendes let the briefcase lie on his knees but made no attempt to open it; he was in no hurry. He waited for the other man to speak.

'So,' Harris said at last, 'what is it you have to sell that could be of interest to me only?'

'Insurance,' Mendes said.

Harris uttered an exclamation of impatience; it might almost have been disappointment, as though he had been expecting something better than this.

'Insurance! Is that all?'

'It is a great deal. No one should be without it.'

'I have all the insurance I need. You had better go now.'

Mendes did not move. 'Ah, but do you have all you need? That is the number one question. I am speaking of life-insurance.'

'I am not interested.'

'Not interested! How can you say that when you know your life is so much in danger?'

Mr Harris looked startled. 'Why do you say that? Why should my life be in danger?'

'Any man with enemies such as you have would be in danger of losing his life.'

'What do you know of my enemies? Who are you?'

Mendes smiled. 'You think my name is not really Smith? Well, you may be right. But yours is not really Harris either, is it?'

'What do you mean?'

'I mean that there is no point in keeping up the pretence for me. I know you too well, Presidente.'

'Presidente!'

'Perhaps I should say ex-Presidente, but it is not important. Señor Harrera will do as well. You are not, I hope, going to deny the fact?'

Harrera seemed about to do so, but then he gave a shrug and appeared to accept the reality of the situation. 'I see that you are a very shrewd man, Mr Smith. Am I to know your correct name also?'

'I think it is better you do not.'

'Better for you?'

'But of course. One has to take precautions. You yourself have taken some: a change of name, a refuge in a distant country. These are not enough perhaps, but that is where I am able to help you. What I am offering is of course not so much life-insurance as life-preservation, which is a somewhat different thing. Life-insurance is of use only to one's heirs and successors; what are called, I believe, the beneficiaries; it does not afford protection.' Mendes patted the briefcase again. 'Now what I have in here could really be described as a life-preserver; it would give you solid protection.'

'You are talking nonsense,' Harrera said. 'What could you have that would protect me? And besides, why should I need protection? My life is not in danger.'

'Oh, surely you don't believe that.'

'Why should I not believe it? Who do you suppose would wish to kill me?'

'Who? Why the man who did his utmost to have you killed when you were escaping, the man who has taken your place as the head of state, the leader of the military junta: General Bernardo Alvarez.'

'He has got what he wanted. I am no threat to him now.'

'He may not believe that. I am not sure that I believe it myself. But I am sure that he would feel safer if you were out of the way for good. While you are alive there is always the possibility of a return.'

'I have no ambitions in that direction.'

'That may be true, but how do you convince him?'

'So you think he will try to kill me?'

'Not personally, of course; he has too much to occupy his time. And why should he bother to do the dirty work himself when he can easily employ agents to do it for him?'

'But how would they find me?'

Mendes smiled. 'I found you, didn't I?'

It had not been easy but he had done it. The contacts had helped, and finally he had succeeded in tracing Harrera to this pleasant house tucked away in a quiet little byway in Hampstead. It was somewhat different from the presidential palace in which he had formerly lived, but perhaps it had its advantages; for a man who was seeking peace and quiet nothing could have been better. And perhaps Harrera really had no desire to go back to the stresses and dangers of political life in a fiery Central American republic.

'They will find you, too, you know.'

'They have not done so yet, and much time has passed since the military coup.'

'But if they want to do it they will not give up. If you believe you are safe here you are living in a fool's paradise. And there is another thing: you haven't got Colonel Rias to help you now.'

Mendes had touched a nerve; Harrera winced visibly. Rias had been more than a friend; he had been a source of confidence, someone to turn to for advice and help, like an elder brother. Rias had been so strong, and now he was dead.

Mendes said softly: 'Would you like to see now what I have to offer you?'

Harrera did not say he would but he did not say he would not. Mendes took his silence for assent. He got up from his chair, carried his briefcase to the table under the window and pushed the clutter of papers to one side. He opened the briefcase and took from it a selection of the photographs he had taken in the Bahamas. He laid them out on the table and stood back to make way for Harrera.

'What do you think of these?'

Harrera looked at the photographs and his mouth tightened. But he said nothing.

'You recognise the two people, of course?' Mendes said. 'You must have seen both of them many times, though not in such a lack of attire.'

Harrera cleared his throat. 'Where did you get these?'

'They were taken by me in the garden of a bungalow in the Bahamas. No one but you and I has ever seen them. I may tell you it almost cost me my life to get them. But what of that?' Mendes shrugged. 'One has to take risks to make an honest living.'

'Why have you brought them to me?'

Mendes stared at Harrera. Could a man who had been his country's president be so stupid that he did not understand what would have been obvious to a child of ten?

'Why have I brought them to you! Don't you see?'

'You had better tell me,' Harrera said.

Mendes told him. 'Can you imagine what would happen if these photographs were to fall into the hands of General Zaragoza? The lady is his wife; he dotes on her. And here she is disporting herself in the nude with his closest friend when she is supposed to be staying with her cousin in Paris. Zaragoza is a jealous man; he is also a violent man. What do you suppose he would do to Alvarez if he were to have knowledge of this liaison?'

'Go on,' Harrera said quietly. 'I see that you have worked this out. Now you are going to tell me what I should do.'

'I don't think I need to tell you, but if you wish me to, I will. You should send copies of the photographs, or at least some of them as samples, to General Alvarez. You should inform him that other copies and the original negatives are lodged in a safe place and that in the event of your meeting your death in any suspicious circumstances your lawyer has instructions to send them to General Zaragoza. That should be sufficient.'

'So you are suggesting that I should resort to blackmail?'

Mendes gave an impatient snap of the fingers. 'Blackmail! What is that? A word.

Why man, your life is at stake. Alvarez has deposed you by force of arms and has already tried to kill you. Why hesitate to take precautions because of a word?'

Harrera was silent; he appeared to be deep in thought.

Mendes said: 'You will not be so foolish as to refuse? You have a daughter. For her sake as well as your own you should do all that is possible to preserve your life.'

'How much,' Harrera said, speaking slowly and as if with some effort, 'are you asking for these?' He indicated the photographs with a fluttering gesture of the fingers which seemed to register a kind of distaste.

Mendes did not immediately name a price. He said: 'For such merchandise you must expect to pay generously. The difficulty of obtaining them must be taken into account. The risk.'

'I am not a rich man.'

Mendes's face registered disbelief. 'You had three years in office. Are you telling me that in that time you failed to put money into a Swiss bank account?'

'Some men might have done so. I did not.'

Mendes was astounded that anyone should have been so honest—so stupid indeed—as to allow such a golden opportunity to pass by without making full use of it. But perhaps Harrera possessed enough wealth anyway and could afford to ignore the chance of milking the public purse. His statement that he was not a rich man was probably nothing more than a bargaining ploy.

'I think you are not poor,' Mendes said.

'The term is relative. What is your price?'

'I think twenty thousand would not be unreasonable.'

'Twenty thousand in what currency?'

'The currency of this country we are in now.'

'Twenty thousand pounds! It's out of the question.'

'It is not a great price to pay for a shield against sudden death.'

'Perhaps. But as I told you, I am not a rich man.'

Mendes looked at him reflectively. Then he said: 'Make me an offer.'

Harrera thought about it for half a minute. 'I could possibly manage ten thousand.'

Finally he agreed to manage fifteen thousand. Mendes was not dissatisfied; he had been prepared to settle for less; he had been stuck with the photographs for too long for his liking. Fifteen grand was a fair price, all things considered.

'It will have to be cash, of course. In a case like this I prefer not to bother with cheques.'

'Then I'm afraid you'll have to wait a day or two. I don't keep that kind of money on hand.'

Mendes was not worried. What difference did a few more days make? It was some time since he had last been in London and there was plenty to do by way of passing the idle hours. Besides, there might be subjects for his camera.

'I'll call again the day after tomorrow. Will that be all right?'

Harrera said it would. 'You'll bring all the photographs, won't you? The negatives as well.'

Mendes promised that Harrera would have the lot.

When he had gone Harrera sat in a chair and thought about the deal he had just made. He felt soiled, as though he had been handling dirt. He would never have imagined he could sink so low as to employ such means as these. Admittedly he was dealing with a man who had used illegal methods to oust him from office, a man who had tried to kill him and would not hesitate to try again if given half a chance; a man, moreover, who was not above seducing his friend's wife. So was it not perfectly in order to use any kind of weapon to defend oneself against such a villain? Perhaps.

But Harrera had always prided himself on being an honourable man, and argue how he might, this action he was contemplating was not honourable. Yet he knew that he would take it, because he did not wish to go in continual fear of his life. And also because he had a daughter.

He felt dirty, nevertheless. He went to the

bathroom and washed his hands, but the dirt remained.

*   *   *

Mendes returned at the time and on the day when he had said he would. He drove his rented car up the drive between the lawns and the flower-beds, parked it outside the front door of the square Georgian house with its pale weathered bricks and virginia creeper and rang the bell. The housekeeper, Mrs Higgs, recognising him this time, let him in at once and ushered him into the library-cum-study where Harrera was waiting.

· 'You have brought them all?' Harrera asked. 'You have kept none for your own use?'

Mendes looked pained. 'Now would I do a thing like that? Don't you trust me?'

Harrera trusted Mendes only because he was forced to. He took the money from a drawer and placed the bundles of notes on the table by the window. Mendes opened the briefcase he had again brought with him and extracted the prints and negatives.

'There are two copies of each picture. I don't suppose you wanted more?'

'No,' Harrera said. 'Two will be ample.'

Mendes started putting the money into the briefcase.

'You're not going to count it?' Harrera asked.

61

Mendes smiled. 'No need to do that. A man like you I know wouldn't cheat me. You're an honourable gentleman, Señor Presidente.'

'And yet what I am proposing to do is neither honourable nor gentlemanly.'

'It's necessary; that's what's important. When you're dealing with swine you have to adopt the manners of the pig-trough.'

Before he left Mendes offered to shake hands with Harrera, but Harrera pretended not to notice the gesture; he had no wish to touch Mendes's hand.

'Well,' Mendes said, 'goodbye, Señor Presidente.'

'Don't call me that,' Harrera said.

'No? Then goodbye, Mr Harris. Maybe we'll meet again some day. Maybe we'll do a bit more business.'

'I think not,' Harrera said. He wanted to do no more business with Mendes. He hoped he would never again set eyes on the man who called himself Mr Smith.

When Mendes had gone he took two of the photographs and locked the rest of them away for the present in a drawer. He then sat down and wrote a letter to General Alvarez, worded more or less as Mendes had suggested. After he had addressed the envelope he marked it clearly: 'Private and confidential. For the attention of General Alvarez only.' As an extra precaution he put the photographs in a smaller envelope, sealed it and marked it in the same way. He put the smaller envelope and the letter inside the larger one and sealed it carefully. Later that day he sent it off by air mail. He returned home and made a telephone call to the solicitor who handled his affairs.

*   *   *

When Alvarez opened the envelope that had come by air mail from England he read the letter and looked at the photographs. The colour rose to his cheeks and he frowned heavily. Then he began to march back and forth in the private office which he had inherited from the man who had written the letter, cursing savagely.

After about ten minutes he felt calm enough to act in a normal manner, and he then sent for Captain Alberto Velasco, who was his nephew and the only man of all those around him whom he completely trusted.

Velasco came at once. Alvarez did not show him the photographs but told him about them in a guarded way. He also gave Velasco certain instructions which the young captain understood perfectly.

'You will leave without delay,' Alvarez said. 'You may take one man with you, someone trustworthy; but do not tell him more than is absolutely necessary. Tell him nothing of the nature of these.' He touched the envelope in which he had replaced the incriminating photographs. 'You understand?'

'I understand,' Velasco said. His eyes met those of his uncle, and Alvarez saw in them a steeliness that matched his own.

'Act in this matter with discretion, Alberto, but do not fail me. The result could be rapid promotion and more besides.'

Velasco nodded. 'I shall do my utmost to justify your faith in me. I promise you I shall not fail.'

CHAPTER SIX

CHINK IN THE ARMOUR

It took Captain Velasco very little time to make contact with Harrera. The task had been made easy for him by the fact that Harrera had revealed his address in the letter to General Alvarez. With the protection provided by the photographs he deemed it no longer necessary to keep his whereabouts a secret. Besides, as Mendes had said, they would have traced him eventually anyway.

Velasco called in the afternoon without an appointment. Mrs Higgs, as she had done with Mendes, left him waiting on the doorstep while she went to see whether Mr Harris would see him. Harrera said he would; he knew who Velasco was and it did not surprise him that Alvarez should have sent his nephew. He was interested to hear what the captain would have to propose, but he felt no apprehension; the strength of his own position ensured that he had nothing to fear.

Harrera was in the room where he had made his deal with Mendes when Mrs Higgs ushered Velasco in.

'Good afternoon,' Harrera said. 'Won't you sit down?'

Velasco made a slight bow and accepted a chair. He was extremely well dressed in a grey two-piece suit and his shoes were highly polished. There was in fact an overall polish about his appearance. Looking at him, Harrera could detect echoes of Alvarez: the athletic physique, the dark handsome features, the elegance, the hardness in the eyes. Velasco was only in his late twenties, but he had packed a wealth of experience into his brief life, not all of it greatly to his credit.

As a very young army officer before the Harrera government came to power he had seen a good deal of active service against the guerrillas and had employed particularly savage methods to combat them. There were many villages that had cause to remember with bitterness the activities of Velasco's men. As a junior officer he had not of course instituted the barbarous methods employed to deter the peasants from lending aid to the left-wing guerrillas; he was simply carrying out orders.

But he carried them out with enthusiasm and a lust for brutality and slaughter that made his name a byword before he had reached the age of twenty-five.

Harrera knew all this, and he could not avoid looking closely at his visitor, as though trying to penetrate the urbane and civilised exterior and reach the vicious sadist he suspected was hidden beneath. During his term as president he would have liked to bring men like Velasco to trial, charging them with crimes against the people; but the army had been too powerful; it closed ranks and protected its own. Even a democratically elected head of government could do nothing against the military; he had been forced to temporise, and in the end even temporising had been of no avail.

'We have met before, I think,' Velasco said. 'Though you may not remember so unimportant a person.' There was a false modesty in the words which did not deceive Harrera. Velasco certainly did not regard himself as being unimportant.

Harrera remembered perfectly. 'You misjudge me, Captain Velasco. I may be growing old but I assure you my memory is still excellent. You were introduced to me by your uncle, General Alvarez. I trust the general is well?'

Velasco gave a smile, the cynical nature of which he made no attempt to disguise. 'He was in excellent health when I last saw him. A shade troubled in the mind, perhaps.'

'Yes?'

'Concerning the matter of some photographs, I understand.'

Harrera wondered whether Velasco had been shown the photographs, but he did not ask. He marvelled at the confidence which Alvarez must have in the young man; he would have expected the general to keep the secret of the photographs locked in his own head. But perhaps it was not in the nature of the man to accept the situation passively; every instinct must have urged him to take action; and the tool he had chosen—one might rather call it the weapon—was Velasco. Harrera had no illusions regarding the deadly nature of that weapon, and in spite of himself he felt a chill in the spine, a slight tremor of fear. But he had control of his voice as he said:

'General Alvarez is troubled by some photographs?'

'Troubled is perhaps too strong a word for what he feels. A sense of incompleteness would be nearer the mark.'

'I don't quite understand. Please explain.'

'He has two photographs; they are part of a set. The general has a desire to possess the complete set.'

'An understandable desire. The photographs are valuable, perhaps?'

'That is a matter of opinion. To the general

I believe they have great sentimental value. As mementoes of a very happy period in his life, you understand?'

'I understand. Though I have to confess that of all the men I have ever met General Alvarez is the one whom I would least suspect of being influenced by sentiment.'

Velasco smiled again. 'Possibly you misjudge him.'

'Possibly,' Harrera said drily.

'In order to complete the set,' Velasco went on, 'he is prepared to pay a generous price.'

'And he has authorised you to make the purchase?'

'That is so.'

'Supposing you were to be told that the photographs are not for sale. What then?'

'It would be a great disappointment. But there is a price for all things.'

'There is no price for which a man would be prepared to sell his life. No cash price, that is. He might give it away for a cause or a friend, but that is a different thing.'

Velasco was silent for a while, gazing at Harrera in a reflective manner, as though sizing up an opponent in a single combat. Then he said:

'Shall we stop talking in this roundabout way? We both know that you are the man who has the photographs which General Alvarez so dearly wants. We both know that they were taken by a sneak photographer in the Bahamas and portray him and a certain lady in compromising circumstances.'

'If frankness is to be the order between us,' Harrera said, 'let us not be mealy-mouthed and talk about compromising circumstances. Let us state the facts bluntly: General Alvarez and the lady were bathing naked and acting towards each other with a considerable degree of intimacy. Let us state also that the lady in question was the wife of General Mateo Zaragoza.'

He was watching Velasco closely and he would have made a guess that some at least of what he had said was news to the young man. Perhaps Alvarez had not named the lady; perhaps also he had not revealed that the party of two had been in the nude. But Velasco was only momentarily taken out of his stride. He spoke coolly.

'Very well; let us agree that that is the long and the short of it. The fact remains that General Alvarez desires the pictures and will pay handsomely for them. He has authorised me to say that he will give you anything within reason for all the prints and negatives.'

'They are not for sale. Do you imagine I would part with the only shield I have against the knife or bullet of the assassin?'

'He has also authorised me to give you his solemn promise that you will come to no harm. If you let him have the photographs you can live in peace, in the knowledge that he has no

69

evil designs against you.'

Harrera smiled wryly. 'You must forgive me if I prefer the safeguard of retaining the photographs to any reliance I might put on the promises of a military dictator of doubtful morals.'

Velasco frowned. He seemed at last to be losing some of his coolness. He said: 'There may be ways of making you change your mind. Perhaps I should tell you that I have not come to this country alone. There is a man with me who is well practised in the art of persuading people to do what they have no inclination to do. His name is Diego Guayama.'

Harrera could not avoid giving a slight start. Sergeant Guayama was notorious as an interrogator; he was a torturer, ruthless, implacable, a man who delighted in inflicting pain. And this brutal soldier Velasco had brought with him on his errand of persuasion. Well, it was only to be expected; for Guayama had been in Velasco's unit in the fighting against the guerrillas and the two of them had worked hand-in-glove in their bloody operations.

'I see that you know who I am talking about,' Velasco said.

'You are threatening me with torture? You seem to forget that you are not still in Central America. They order things differently here. There are laws.'

'So you think the British police will protect

70

you? How can they? Do you suppose they would put a guard on this house if you asked them? It is hardly likely.'

Harrera knew that what Velasco had said was true; he could not look to the police for protection; he had no proof that he was being threatened. But he still held the trump card.

'What advantage would you gain from torturing me? If I give you the photographs I am giving away my life. Torture will not persuade me to do that.'

'Perhaps you overestimate your own powers of resistance to pain. There might come a time when death would seem the easier way.'

'I do not think so,' Harrera said. He hoped he was convincing Velasco, for he was not sure he could bear torture. Perhaps he ought to go into hiding as soon as Velasco left. But he was reluctant to do that; it was the very kind of thing he had bought the photographs in order to avoid.

Further discussion between the two men was interrupted at that moment by the opening of the door. Margarita came in and stopped suddenly when she saw Velasco.

'Oh, I'm sorry. I didn't know you had a visitor.'

Velasco had risen from his chair. Reluctantly Harrera made the introduction.

'Captain Velasco, this is my daughter Margarita.'

Velasco looked at the girl in undisguised

admiration. 'I am charmed, Señorita.'

She showed surprise at the word. They had been speaking in English. 'Señorita!'

'The captain is a compatriot,' Harrera explained quickly. He wished the girl had not chosen that moment to come into the room; he had had no desire that she should meet Velasco or that he should see her. Somehow, he had a sense of foreboding, a feeling that no good would come of the encounter. 'Captain Velasco knows who I am.'

Margarita glanced inquiringly at Velasco, and he answered the unspoken question. 'I happened to be in this country and it seemed only courteous to pay a call on such a distinguished exile.' He did not explain how he had found where Harrera was living and she did not ask, though the thought might have been in her mind.

She said: 'So this is purely a social visit?'

Velasco made a slight gesture of the hand. 'There is a small matter of business also.'

'You make it sound of no importance.'

Velasco shrugged.

Harrera said: 'I think it will be better if you leave us now. Captain Velasco will wish to finish his business and be on his way. I am sure he is a busy man.'

It was an order, and the girl left the room.

Velasco remarked: 'You have a very attractive daughter.'

'People have said so.'

72

'I had forgotten just how attractive. It is some time since I last saw her, and then only at a distance. She has grown in beauty with the years.'

'We will not speak about it,' Harrera said. 'You did not come here to discuss the physical appearance of my daughter.'

'True.' Velasco had sat down again and seemed at ease. 'But it could be an interesting subject. No doubt you have a great affection for her. Is it not so?'

'It would be an unnatural thing if I did not, seeing that she is my own child.'

'Of course. And you would not wish her to come to any harm, I imagine.'

'I can see no reason why any harm should come to her,' Harrera said. But he could. He would have had to be singularly obtuse not to have realised what Velasco was hinting at.

'And there need be no reason,' Velasco said, 'if you act intelligently. I would say it is very much in your power to protect her from any unpleasantness.'

'You would not dare to touch her.' Harrera was restraining his anger with difficulty. He had always been a man of peace, but at that moment he could have killed Velasco without compunction. 'You would not dare to lay a finger on her.'

Velasco was cool. 'There are few things I would not dare to do. You know my reputation; judge from that. As to laying a

73

finger on the charming Margarita, I think it might be more pleasant to do so in the act of love than of torture. Of course men have been known to do both, the one after the other. Sergeant Guayama for example; now there is a man of the most singular tastes. You should talk to him one of these days; you would find it a most interesting experience, I assure you.'

'Get out,' Harrera said, choking. 'Leave this house immediately.'

Velasco stood up languidly. 'Well, I will go. I will give you a day or two to think over what I have said, and when you have considered everything carefully I am sure you will be prepared to conclude a deal in the matter of the photographs.'

'You are despicable.' Harrera's hands were shaking; there was an uncontrollable tic in his left cheek. 'Utterly despicable.'

'Of course,' Velasco said with complete imperturbability. 'That is one of my most valuable qualities.' He smoothed out the slight creases in his jacket. 'I shall take the liberty of calling on you again very shortly.'

When he had left Harrera stood for some time staring bleakly out of the window and striving to recover some degree of composure. He was deeply worried now. He had been consoling himself ever since the visit of Pedro Mendes and the posting of the letter to General Alvarez with the thought that, distasteful though the business might be, he could now rest easy in his mind regarding any possible attempt on his life. He had, so he believed, effectively spiked the general's guns.

Now, however, he saw that he had been living in a fool's paradise; he had failed to see the weakness of his position, failed to appreciate the fact that there was a hostage to fortune living with him in the house. But it had not been lost on Velasco; one glance at Margarita, and like the cunning tactician that he was, he had recognised the advantage that fate had presented to him.

So, Harrera thought, he must be robbed of that advantage. And there was no time to waste, for he was not a man to let the grass grow under his feet. Moreover, he had that butcher Guayama with him. The ice was in Harrera's spine again as he pictured Margarita in the hands of that degenerate. Such a possibility must be eliminated at any cost.

He heard the door open behind him, and when he turned he saw that Margarita was there again.

'I saw Captain Velasco going away,' she said. 'This business he came to discuss with you; don't you think I ought to be told about it? I am not a child, you know.'

'Yes,' Harrera said. 'I have been turning the matter over in my mind and I think you are entitled to know. Particularly since it appears that you have now become involved.'

She looked surprised. 'I?'

'Yes. I fear that because of certain actions which I have taken recently you have become endangered. I regret this deeply, and I think I need hardly assure you that I would not have allowed the situation to arise if I could have foreseen what might happen. Now it will be necessary to take steps to repair the damage.'

'I'm afraid I don't follow you,' the girl said. 'Wouldn't it be better if you started at the beginning and told me what this is all about?'

Harrera gave a sigh. 'Yes, that is what I had better do. There is much that is distasteful about it and I would have preferred to keep it from you, but I see that it is now not possible to do so. I will tell you the whole story and then I will suggest what you should do. It may not be quite according to your wishes, but I feel sure that you will see that it is necessary. Sit down, my dear.'

She sat down and waited for him to begin. He hesitated a few moments, as though still reluctant to get down to it, but finally, standing with his back to the writing-table and the window, he made a start.

'Last week,' he said, 'I received a visit from a man calling himself Mr Smith—'

CHAPTER SEVEN

UNOFFICIAL ASSIGNMENT

'I want you to meet someone, Sam,' the girl said. 'I'm sure you'll find you have a lot in common.'

Sam Grant doubted it. It had been his experience that whenever he was introduced to people with the assurance that he had a lot in common with them it usually turned out that about all they had in common was the weather. And not always that.

The girl's name was Cynara; which was a name he had always imagined occurred only in a poem by Ernest Dowson. But perhaps her parents had been Dowson lovers at the time of her birth and thought that some day someone might be faithful to her in his fashion. Anyway, it was a nice name and she was a nice girl, and if it came to the point Grant thought he himself might take a stab at being faithful to her if she gave him half a chance, even though he was maybe a dozen years older than she was and not half as nice.

Cynara Jones was twenty-two and had red hair and long legs and freckles, and Grant had met her when working on a case involving some stuff that had gone missing from a Chelsea antique shop. The police had their hands so fully occupied with the metropolitan crime wave that they had given only half-hearted attention to the matter and the owner of the shop had decided to bring in outside help.

Grant, more by good luck than anything else, had managed to recover the stolen articles, and in the course of so doing had become acquainted with Miss Jones, who had at that time been working in the shop. Rather to his surprise the relationship between them had progressed in a highly satisfactory fashion. Cynara seemed to be much attracted to him; he was not sure why, but he did not bother to ask because it seemed to be more sensible to accept the fact and make the most of it.

For his part he had to admit that he was hooked; indeed, he could not remember being so well and truly in the net since the unfortunate death of Miss Susan Sims had left such a gaping hole in his life.

If he had not been so thoroughly taken with Miss Jones he would never have allowed her to drag him along to this party, which was not really his thing at all; it was too crowded, too noisy and crammed with people he didn't know and was not at all sure he wanted to know. It was taking place in a poky little flat above the antique shop where Cynara, for reasons which had not been made quite clear to him, was no longer working. In fact, she was not at that moment working anywhere and he supposed she was drawing money from the

State to keep her going while she looked round for something else.

When she had brought up the subject of the party and suggested that he should go along with her he had raised objections.

'But I haven't been invited.'

'Oh, don't be so stuffy,' she said. 'If I take you along it'll be okay. Not invited indeed! I don't know where you get these crazy old-fashioned ideas.'

'Maybe it was the way I was brought up,' Grant said. 'Anyway, I'm not sure I want to go to any party. Why don't we just go for a drink in a quiet little pub or take in a film or something?'

'Because I want to go to the party and I want you to go with me. It'll take you out of yourself.'

'I don't want to be taken out of myself. I like it in here.'

'You're being very stubborn,' she said. 'I'd have thought you'd have been pleased to go anywhere with me. But of course if you'd rather spend the evening by yourself, o-blooming-kay; you do that.'

'Are you saying that if I don't go with you you'll go alone?'

'You bet your sweet life it's what I'm saying. And I may find somebody else there who doesn't raise all sorts of objections when I suggest doing anything.'

'That's blackmail,' Grant said.

'Is it? Well, you're the legal expert, so I'll take your word for it.'

He wondered why she was so dead keen on his going along with her to the party; she seemed to be making a big thing of it. And in the end of course she got her way; it had been inevitable. Now when she said there was someone she wanted him to meet he had a feeling that he knew the reason for it all; this was the real purpose for which she had dragged him there; it had all been part of a plan she had been turning over in her mind.

'You conned me,' he said.

She gazed at him with her innocent blue eyes. 'Conned you, Sam?'

'You had this in mind all along. You didn't bring me here to take me out of myself; you brought me to meet this person.'

'Well, yes,' she admitted, 'there was that, too. But I knew you'd enjoy yourself once you got here.'

'I'm not enjoying myself. I'm far too hot and the stereo is damaging my eardrums.' He had to raise his voice almost to a shout to make himself heard above the din; but as everyone else seemed to be shouting like a boilermaker it was hardly likely to be noticed.

'Don't be so anti-social,' she said. 'Do you want to meet him or don't you?'

'Do I want to meet who?'

'Whom. And his name is Edgar Wright. I'm sure you'll like him; he's an angel.'

'Well,' Grant said, 'it'll make a change. I don't mix much with the heavenly host. But I still don't want to meet him.'

'I'll fetch him,' she said; and she pushed her way into the scrum, head down and elbows working.

Grant found himself hemmed into a corner by a large woman with a crow's-nest hair-do and a plate of sandwiches.

'Do have one,' she said. 'They're delicious.'

'What's in them?'

'Crab. That's if it isn't minced chicken.'

Grant took one of the sandwiches, which turned out to be cheese.

'Gorgeous party,' the woman said. The amount of brassware hung round her neck would have done credit to a brewer's dray-horse in an agricultural show. 'Are you enjoying yourself?'

'I'm having the time of my life.'

'Jolly good. I always say Brenda's parties are out of this world.'

'Who's Brenda?' Grant asked; but she was not listening.

'Have another sandwich,' she said.

Grant took another sandwich. It seemed to be an order and not to be disobeyed.

'Well, I'll have to be going,' the woman said. 'Must circulate, you know.' She moved away, jingling.

Miss Jones returned dragging Edgar Wright behind her. She introduced him.

'Cynara tells me you're an angel,' Grant said. 'You don't look like one to me, but of course I'm not an expert on the subject.'

Wright gave an embarrassed laugh. He was a rather beefy young man with decently trimmed fair hair and no moustache or beard. He had solid good looks and would have slotted neatly enough into practically any rugby fifteen or rowing eight.

'She exaggerates,' he said.

'Yes, it's something I've noticed. She told me you and I would find we have a lot in common. Do you think we have?'

Wright looked at Grant warily, as though half suspecting that he was being ribbed. 'Well,' he said, 'I don't know about that. It depends, doesn't it?'

'On what?'

'On all sorts of things. I mean I don't really know what you're interested in, do I?'

'You have a point there. And I don't know what you're interested in.'

'He's interested in talking to you,' Cynara said. 'And why have you got two sandwiches?'

'They were forced on me by a large female wearing a black dress and horse-brasses.'

'Some people have all the luck. Nobody's offered me any food and I'm starving.'

'Would you like one of these sandwiches? Preferably the one I haven't bitten.'

'What's in it?'

'The one I've started eating is cheese. I

don't know what the other is.'

'I'll take a chance.' She accepted the unused sandwich and took a bite out of it. 'Ugh! It's crab. I hate crab; it brings me out in bumps.' She dumped the sandwich on a convenient window-sill.

Grant turned to Edgar Wright. 'Why are you interested in me? I'm not famous, you know.'

'I want to have a talk with you.'

'That's what Cynara said. Fire away, then.'

'Don't you think we could go where there isn't so much noise? This isn't quite the place.'

'That's a good idea,' Cynara said. 'We've had enough of this party, haven't we, Sam?'

'I'd had enough of it before I came,' Grant said.

'Let's go, then.'

They took no leave of their hosts. Cynara said it was not necessary and they were probably in the kitchen making more crab sandwiches to poison the guests. They came out into the street and she suggested that they should find a nice quiet little pub.

'It's what I wanted to do in the first place,' Grant said.

'Yes, but it was no good then because Edgar wouldn't have been with us. And he's the one it's all in aid of.'

Wright looked embarrassed again. 'It was your idea. You said it would be all right.'

'And so it is. Come along.'

Ten minutes later they were sitting round a small table with three glasses of beer in front of them, and it was so quiet they could have conversed in whispers. Some people were playing darts on the other side of the room and they could hear the thudding as the points went into the board. There were no pintables and no television, and nobody was playing a piano or singing. It was ideal for a bit of civilised conversation.

'So what do you want to talk to me about?' Grant asked.

'He wants you to do some work for him,' Cynara said.

'Work! What kind of work?'

'Why, the kind you do, of course. Detection, inquiry, sleuthing, that sort of thing. What else did you think it would be?'

'I hadn't thought about it. Anyway, I can't do it, whatever it is.'

'Why not?' Wright said; and he looked a trifle crestfallen. 'You are a private eye, aren't you? Cynara said you were.'

'Not as private as all that. My name isn't Spade, you know. I work for a firm called the Peking Inquiry Agency. I have to do what I'm told to do.'

Wright looked at him in amazement. 'Are you telling me the Chinese have a detective agency in this country?'

Grant answered the question patiently; he had heard it all before. 'It's not Chinese. It's run by a man named Alexander Peking, and if you want my services you have to go and ask him.'

'Oh, Sam,' Cynara said, 'you don't have to be as conscientious as all that. You can do a bit of work on the side. Everybody does it these days; it's called moonlighting.'

'I know what it's called, but I don't happen to go in for that sort of thing.'

'So what you're telling me,' Wright said, 'is that I should go to see your Mr Peking?'

'That's the way it should be done. But I ought to warn you he charges high fees.'

'Oh,' Wright said; and he sounded none too happy about it. 'Is that so?'

'You were thinking about a cut-price service, maybe?'

Wright made no answer to that; he just bit his lip.

'Anyway,' Grant said, 'even if you went to Mr Peking and were prepared to pay his price, you wouldn't get me for the job; not for a couple of weeks, that is. I start my holiday tomorrow.'

'Do you really?' the girl said. 'You didn't tell me that.'

'I didn't know about it until this morning. The old bastard sprang it on me. He said there was nothing much for me to do at the moment and I'd better take my holiday right away, because things would probably start hotting up again before long.'

'Oh,' she said, looking at him thoughtfully. 'And what are you planning to do on this holiday?'

'I haven't got anything planned; there's been no time. That's the devil of it.'

She gave a snap of the fingers. 'Everything's fine, then. You can do this little job for Edgar.'

'Oh, I can, can I? Oddly enough, that isn't quite my idea of a delightful holiday.'

'Now don't be horrid. You needn't be working at it all the time. And I could help you. We could do it together.'

'Do I understand that you're proposing to share my holiday with me?'

'Well, don't you think it's a good idea?'

He thought about it, and it certainly did have considerable attraction.

'I mean it would hardly be like real work, would it?' she said. 'Not with me around. It would be fun.'

He could see how it might be at that. He remembered another girl with red hair who had travelled across America with him to give him a hand with a case he was working on. Her name was Miranda, and that had been fun, too—in parts. In other parts it had been no fun at all, just mean and brutal and bloody; and Miranda had ended up dead. He hoped it was not a precedent or anything like that; but there was no reason why it should be.

He looked at Wright. 'What is this job you want me to do?'

'Well,' Wright said, 'it has to do with a girl named Margarita Harris.'

'How does it have to do with her?'

'I want you to find her.'

'Oh, God!' Grant said. 'Not another missing person, for Pete's sake.'

He had been looking for a girl that other time in America, and Miranda had offered to help him find her; so there was another parallel. He felt a sudden chill in the spine, and he looked at Cynara and thought it was time to call a halt before he was pulled in deeper.

'What do you mean, another missing person?' Wright asked.

'I mean they're poison. For me, anyway. Why don't you go to the Salvation Army?'

'Now you're being silly,' Cynara said.

'I'd be silly to get myself mixed up in this.'

'So you don't want to spend your holiday with me?'

'You're blackmailing me again,' Grant said. 'All right, Edgar, let's hear all about it. Who is this girl and how long has she been missing?'

'Like I said, her name is Margarita Harris and she's been gone three days.'

'Three days! Is that all?'

'It's been a long time for me. I'm in love with her.'

'That figures. Is she in love with you?'

'I think so.'

'You mean you aren't sure?'

'Yes, I am sure,' Wright said. 'She's told me so.'

'Well, it's not proof, but it's evidence. Has she got a family?'

'There's no mother, but she's been living with her father in a house in Hampstead.'

'And have you asked him where she's gone?'

'Of course I have, but he won't tell me.'

'Does he think she's missing?'

'Oh, no; he says he knows where she is.'

'But he still won't tell you?'

'No.'

'Any idea why?'

'I've got a pretty good idea. I think the fact of the matter is he sent her away so she wouldn't see any more of me. I don't think he approves of our relationship.'

'Why wouldn't he do that? At a glance I'd have said you were perfectly acceptable as a prospective son-in-law. I take it your intention is to marry the girl?'

'Of course. As soon as the financial situation makes it possible.'

'So you're not loaded?'

'Not exactly.'

'Well, I'd hardly have called that a sufficient reason for Mr Harris to banish his daughter from your sight. It sounds rather Victorian to me.'

'No, but you know what these Latin Americans are like.'

'Are you telling me Mr Harris is a Latin

American? The name doesn't sound very Spanish.'

'That's because it's not his real name. Margarita told me it's really Harrera, but that's a secret.'

'Not much of a secret if she told you.'

'I think she meant me to keep it to myself. I may be betraying her trust by telling you, but you need to know all the facts if you're going to find her for me, don't you?'

'I haven't said I'll do it. It sounds crazy to me.'

'It's not crazy at all,' Cynara said. 'It's perfectly understandable that Edgar should want to find the girl he's in love with.'

'What is she like?' Grant asked.

'She's an angel,' Cynara said.

'It sounds a perfect match, then. But it's not much of a description, is it?'

Wright pulled a wallet from his pocket and extracted a photograph which he handed to Grant. 'That's Margarita. It's just a snapshot of course, but it's a good likeness.'

Grant looked at the photograph, and he could see why Wright should have been in love with the girl; she was attractive enough to make any man fall in love with her; young, black-haired and lovely.

'How did you come to meet her?'

'It was at art class.'

'Oh, you're an art student?'

'Only evenings. In the daytime I work in a

89

bank.'

'You'll probably make more money that way. May I keep this photograph for the present?'

'Of course.'

'You've no idea where she may have gone?'

'Not a clue. We were going to meet at the art class three evenings ago and then go somewhere afterwards. But she didn't turn up. There was no message or anything. I rang up the house, but I just got Mr Harris on the phone and he said I couldn't speak to Margarita. And then he said she'd gone away.'

'He didn't say for how long?'

'Indefinitely.'

'I think it's disgraceful,' Cynara said.

It was not the word Grant would have used. But he did think it odd. The girl in the photograph looked spirited enough to stand up for herself; yet if Wright's theory was correct it seemed that she had quietly obeyed her father's order and gone away without even getting in touch with the man she loved.

'You'd better give me Mr Harris's address,' he said. 'I'll see what I can do. I'm not promising anything, but I'll look around.'

Cynara leaned over the table and gave him a hug and a kiss. Which was slightly embarrassing in public, but nice.

'I knew you would, Sam. You're a darling. And don't worry, Edgar; I'm sure we'll find her.'

Wright himself looked relieved. He evidently had a touching faith in the professional touch, which Grant hoped would not prove misplaced. After he had written down Mr Harris's address they finished up their drinks and left the public-house. Wright said he had better be going, and they watched him walk away.

'Do you want to go back to the party?' Cynara asked.

'Not particularly.'

'Then why don't you take me back to my place and I'll pick up my gear.'

'What gear?'

'My luggage and stuff.'

'And then what?'

'Then we'll take it to your place, of course.'

'You mean you're moving in with me?'

'Well, that was the plan, wasn't it?'

'If you say so.'

'Don't you want me to?'

'You bet I want you to. I just didn't know if you really meant it.'

'That's okay then. Everything's packed and ready. I've told the other girls I'll be clearing out; it would have been difficult paying my share of the rent now that I'm out of a job. They don't mind; they've got someone else lined up to take my place.'

'You mean it's all arranged? But you didn't know you'd be moving until this evening.'

'That's what you think,' she said.

CHAPTER EIGHT

COINCIDENCE

Cynara insisted on cooking bacon and eggs in the kitchenette. She was a healthy English girl and she said she liked to start the day with a solid English breakfast; she was not one for a nibble of raw carrot and a swig of orange juice.

'Besides,' she said, 'we've got work to do and we need to kick off on the right foot, don't we?'

Grant wondered how she managed to look so bright and fresh at that time in the morning. He himself felt a trifle bleary-eyed and generally frayed round the edges; but perhaps that was just the gap in their ages making itself felt. One thing he had to admit was that the somewhat tatty flat in Camden Town had not looked so good since Susan Sims had ceased to share it with him. Cynara was not much like the late Miss Sims in appearance, but she had the same effect of lending a touch of enchantment to otherwise pretty ordinary and even squalid surroundings.

They ate at the counter in the kitchenette, sitting elbow-to-elbow on high stools. Cynara was wearing a pair of faded jeans and a white T-shirt with a picture of the Taj Mahal on the front; she had done nothing to the red hair except give it a shake and a couple of strokes with a brush, and it looked just fine.

'I suppose the first thing to do,' she said, 'is to go out to Hampstead and give Mr Harris-Harrera a thorough grilling.'

'Grilling is hardly the word. He's not a criminal being interrogated by the police, you know. We shall have to tread lightly. I'll ask him a few questions, but it'll probably be unproductive. If he wouldn't tell Edgar where his daughter is, there's no reason why he should be any more forthcoming with us.'

'Except that he sent her away to stop her seeing Edgar and wouldn't be likely to tell him anything.'

'We don't know he sent her away for that reason. It's only a conjecture.'

'Well, have you any likelier theory?'

'Not at the moment, but I'm keeping an open mind.'

'He must be a horrible man,' Cynara said. It was evident that she had already closed hers.

*   *   *

They drove out to Hampstead in the Maestro with which Mr Peking had been persuaded somewhat reluctantly to replace the ageing Cortina that Grant had previously used. It was a pleasant morning and would have been just right for a trip to the seaside if there had not been other things to do.

93

Grant had thought of telephoning Mr Harris but had decided that a face-to-face talk would be more likely to bring forth information; it was too easy for a man to break off a telephone conversation if he felt like doing so. There was no guarantee that Harris would be at home; they were just taking the chance that he might be; if he was not, nothing would be lost except a little time. And as it turned out he was at home, and after Mrs Higgs had kept them waiting for a while on the doorstep she came back to say that Mr Harris would see them.

They were shown into the room with the bookshelves and the writing-table, and Harrera looked at them inquiringly. Grant's first impression was that he was a sick man; his complexion was muddy and there were dark pouches under his eyes; he could have been sleeping poorly and maybe worrying about something.

'I don't know what it is you wish to see me about,' he said, 'but you had better sit down.' He indicated chairs with a flutter of one veiny hand. 'I didn't quite catch the names.'

'My name is Grant and this is Miss Jones.'

Harrera made a slight inclination of the head in the direction of Cynara.

'Miss Jones is a friend of your daughter's,' Grant said.

'Yes?' One of Harrera's eyebrows lifted a little, but he showed no other reaction to the

94

information.

'You may have heard her speak of me,' Cynara said.

'No, I cannot say I have.'

'Well, perhaps she wouldn't; but the point is this, I haven't seen her around for a while and as we were passing this way I thought I might as well call in and see if she's okay.'

'My daughter is perfectly well, thank you.'

'And she's here, is she?'

'No, she is not here at the moment. She is away.'

'Oh, I see. She's on holiday, is she?'

'In a way, yes; you could say that.'

Cynara took a small notebook and pencil from her shoulder-bag. 'I'd like to write to her. Would you give me her address?'

'No,' Harrera said, somewhat sharply, 'that is not possible.'

'Not possible! But why?'

Harrera hesitated; he seemed oddly ill-at-ease. Then he said: 'The fact is she is on the Continent. She will be travelling around, painting, one day here, another day there, not staying in one place for long.'

'You mean you are not in touch with her?'

'She has promised to give me a call by telephone now and then.'

'And you are not worried about her?'

'Worried!' Harrera looked startled. 'Why should I be worried? She is perfectly capable of looking after herself. She has taken her car

95

and is driving around in it. She will put up at hotels along the way. She may stay a little longer in some places than in others.'

Grant had the impression that he was making it up as he went along, adding bits as they came into his head.

'She has been planning this for some time, perhaps?'

'Planning? Oh, yes, for quite a while. She has talked of nothing else.'

They left soon after that. There was nothing more they were likely to get from Harrera, and he seemed impatient for them to go. Mrs Higgs opened the door for them and watched them get into the Maestro and drive away.

'I wonder whether that housekeeper knows anything,' Cynara said.

'It's possible. But somehow I don't think Harrera would take her much into his confidence.'

'Do you believe that story about a painting tour on the Continent?'

'No. It was obvious that he was lying. And we know she hasn't been planning anything of the kind. She would have been bound to tell Edgar if she had.'

'So why make up such a story?'

'To throw us off the track. He doesn't want us to go looking for her.'

'In case we were to tell Edgar where she is? Is that what you mean?'

'Frankly,' Grant said, 'I don't think it has

much to do with Edgar. It's my opinion that if he has sent her away it's for some quite different reason.'

'Like what?'

'I don't know. But I'd like to. This thing begins to be intriguing. And something else has occurred to me. Wasn't there a man named Harrera who was president of some republic in South America or maybe Central America and got turfed out in a military take-over not so very long ago?'

She stared at him. 'You don't think our Mr Harris is that man?'

'I think it's just possible. And if so there could be a lot of other threads we don't know about in this particular piece of Latin American cloth. It could be something quite different from a simple case of young love not running smooth. Mr Harris looked to me like a man who had a lot more on his mind than his daughter's boy-friend.'

'So what do we do now?'

'That's the question. We haven't got much to go on, have we? Got any ideas?'

'You're the professional,' she said complacently. 'I'm depending on you.'

'I may be a professional but I'm not a miracle-worker. What I need is a hint as to where she may have gone. Has she ever said anything to you that might give us a clue?'

'Not that I remember. Though, come to think of it, she did mention a cottage down in

Norfolk.'

'A cottage?'

'Yes. Some place her father saw advertised to let as a rural retreat. She said it seemed to catch his eye because it was near a river and there was fishing, which is something apparently he's always wanted to do and has never had the time for. He's rented it for the rest of the summer. I believe they were planning to go down there soon, and Margarita was going to do some painting. Do you think that's where she can have gone?'

'It seems possible. And it fits in. Mr Harris may have been telling half the truth when he talked about her painting. Do you know where the place is?'

'Well, she did tell me the name of the village, but I've forgotten it.'

'You can't have forgotten,' Grant said. 'It must be in there somewhere. Think.'

'I am thinking, but it's just not there.'

'Concentrate.'

She sat beside him in the car, concentrating for all she was worth. She concentrated so hard he began to think she had gone to sleep. But it all came to nothing.

'Go through the letters of the alphabet. See if that helps.'

She went through the letters slowly. It was no help at all.

'I'm disappointed in you,' Grant said. 'I thought you'd be more helpful than this.'

'I'm doing my best.'

'Well, it's just not good enough, is it?'

'Stop nagging me,' she said. 'Maybe my subconscious will get to work on it and come up with something.'

Grant had a better idea than waiting for her subconscious to deliver the goods. He stopped the car in a quiet side-street and fished out a book of touring maps of the British Isles. Together he and Cynara went systematically over the two pages covering the county of Norfolk, reading the names of the towns and villages.

'That's it,' Cynara said with conviction. Then more doubtfully: 'I think.'

She had her finger on a place named Wendleham, which was to the south-east of Norwich.

'Aren't you sure?' Grant asked.

'Yes, I am. Well, nearly.'

'No more than that?'

'Well, you wouldn't expect me to swear an oath on it, would you? I mean it's impossible to be absolutely certain. If I'd ever seen it written down it would have been easier to remember; but I'm fairly sure. I remember at the time it made me think of Peter Pan.'

'Peter Pan!'

'Wendy, you know. One of the children in the play.'

'You're sure the place wasn't Hookham?'

'You don't have to be sarcastic,' she said.

'Shall we go down there and take a look?'

Grant put the book of maps away. 'I suppose we may as well. But it's a bit late to make a start today. I suggest we go to bed early and set off first thing in the morning.'

'That sounds like a good idea. What do you call going to bed early?'

'Well,' Grant said, 'I think we'd better have lunch first, don't you?'

*   *   *

It was raining when he backed the Maestro out of the lock-up garage where he kept it. As they drove northward the London streets had a grey wet look about them which was hardly calculated to lift the spirits. But Cynara was cheerful.

'It'll clear up pretty soon,' she said. 'The weatherman said it would.'

'I don't believe what weathermen say,' Grant said. 'I think they use a bunch of seaweed and one of those little wooden houses where the woman comes out if it's going to be fine and the man comes out if it's going to be wet.'

'Don't be so gloomy. You're on holiday, remember. Enjoy yourself.'

'You think it's going to be a riot of fun down at Wendleham?'

'There's no telling what it'll be like until we get there.'

'I know what it'll be like,' Grant said. 'I come from that part of the country. I was born in a farmhouse on the borders of Suffolk and Norfolk.'

'Then you should be happy to be returning to the haunts of your youth.'

'The haunts of my youth are no attraction to me on a wet day in June.'

'It'll be a dry day in June before we're there,' Cynara said. 'I promise you.'

She was right at that. It had stopped raining before they reached Hatfield, and at Newmarket the sun was shining warmly and the road was dry.

Cynara crowed. 'I told you so. Doesn't it make you glad to be alive?'

'I always feel glad to be alive,' Grant said. 'I've seen what the other thing looks like.'

It was still quite early in the day when they drove into Wendleham, and the weather had become warm and summery. The village was of a fair size and it seemed to be a thriving place; it had a core of older buildings with some new housing estates that had attached themselves to the perimeter like young limpets.

The river was on the south side and was spanned by an iron bridge; and there was a sluice and a disused water-mill which had been turned into a private residence. On a small square of turf in the centre of the village was a stone cross on the plinth of which were carved

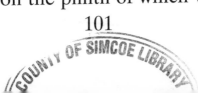

the names of those villagers who had gone away to fight in two world wars and had never come back.

Grant found a place to park the car, and they got out and looked about them.

'I suppose,' Cynara said, 'this is where we start making inquiries.'

'It might be as well,' Grant said. 'I don't think there'd be much point in standing here waiting for Miss Harris to pass by.'

They started with the shops, showing the photograph of the girl and asking if anyone could remember serving her. People looked at the picture and tried to be helpful, but usually it ended in a shake of the head and a regretful admission that they could not remember having seen the young lady. Nor did the name appear to ring any bells. The rather stout woman who was sub-postmistress and proprietress of the general stores thought she might have had a customer who looked a bit like the person in the photograph, but she could not be sure; there were quite a lot of strangers who came in during the summer months.

'Holidaymakers?' asked Grant.

'Some of them are,' the woman said. 'There's people come down from London and the like for a breath of fresh air as you might say. And then there's the camping site only a mile away. A few drift in from there.'

'Do you know of any cottages that are let as

holiday homes?'

The woman gave the question some consideration before answering. But again the result was negative. 'Can't say I do. Though that's not to say there may not be some I don't know about.'

'Thank you,' Grant said. 'You've been very helpful.'

'Wish I could've done more,' the woman said.

When they came out of the general store Grant saw a blue Escort parked on the opposite side of the road. A man came out of a telephone kiosk and got into the car. He did not immediately start it but took a cigarette from a packet and lit it.

'Wait here,' Grant said. 'There's someone over there I'd like to speak to.'

'A friend of yours?'

'I wouldn't call him that.'

The man in the Escort seemed to be unaware of Grant's approach as he crossed the road, but Grant felt sure he had been spotted. The window of the car was down and the man's elbow was resting on the door. He gave an exaggerated start when Grant tapped him on the arm.

'Surprise, surprise,' Grant said. 'Fancy meeting you here.'

'Well, blow me down!' The man turned his head and stared. 'If it ain't Sammy Grant as ever was. What brings you to this neck of the woods? You on a case?'

'No; I happen to be on holiday.'

'Now there's a coincidence,' the man said. He had a pimply face and a fat sagging body inadequately held in check by a brown suit that would have benefited from a visit to the dry-cleaners. 'So am I.'

Grant did not believe him and he was quite sure that the fat man had not believed him either. There was a lot of disbelief floating around.

'Maybe you're waiting for someone,' he suggested.

'No; I'm on my ownsome. Though I see you have a young lady with you. Nice. You're a lucky man, Sammy. Don't know how you do it.' The fat man gave a fat leer which made Grant feel like giving one of his fat ears a tweak. But he restrained himself.

'Well, it's been nice meeting you, Freddy. Like you said, it's a coincidence. If I didn't know you better I might think you've been tailing me.'

'And I might say the same about you. But we both know better than that, don't we?'

'So long,' Grant said. 'Have a good holiday.'

He walked away. The fat man sucked at his cigarette and blew smoke through his nose.

'Who is that man?' Cynara asked.

'His name,' Grant said, 'is Freddy Granger and he's in the same line of business as I am.'

'A private eye! What's he doing here?'

'He says he's on holiday.'

'But you don't believe that, do you?'

'No, I don't believe it. And I'll tell you something about our Mr Granger; he's a loner and he has a bad reputation. He'll take jobs that other agents would never handle; he isn't choosy.'

'So if he isn't on holiday, what is he doing? It's a bit of a coincidence his being here too, isn't it?'

'That's what he said. But I don't think it is a coincidence. At a guess I'd say he's on the same game as we are.'

'Looking for Margarita?'

'Yes.'

'But why?'

'Well, obviously he's working for someone. And if I'm right that means there's someone else who very much wants to get in touch with Miss Harris and is willing to pay Freddy to find her for him.'

'But who would?'

'I don't know, but I have a nasty feeling there could be some kind of Central American connection. It's just a hunch, but I'm beginning to get a whiff of something and it's not the kind of smell I like.'

'But how would he have found this place? Do you think he followed us down from London?'

'No; that's most unlikely. I'm not sure he knows what we're here for, but I'd say he's making a shrewd guess at it.'

'But if he didn't follow us down, how did he get a lead?'

'I've been thinking about that and my guess is the housekeeper. She may have heard the name of the village mentioned by Harrera or Margarita and Freddy may have got on to her. He's as sharp as a pin, even if he's not as straight. A bit of bribery would probably have bought him the information.'

'Well, if so, that would prove we've come to the right village. Do you think he's found the cottage?'

'I don't know, but he's been making a telephone call and I don't much like the look of that.'

'You really do think Margarita is in danger, don't you?'

'Yes, I do.'

Cynara looked worried. 'We'd better be quick about finding her then, hadn't we?'

'Yes,' Grant said, 'I think we had.'

CHAPTER NINE

SWALLOWS

It was Cynara who spotted the notice-board. Until then they had had no luck at all and time was passing. They had been driving around more in hope than expectation, and then about half a mile outside the village on the north side there was a farmhouse and a black barn with a pantiled roof and some outbuildings and a couple of stacks of hay.

There was a crumbling flint wall enclosing the farmyard, with a five-barred gate across the entrance. On the gate was a painted board with a notice which read: 'Black Barn Riding Stables. Penelope Green, prop.'

'Margarita is nuts on horses,' Cynara remarked. 'She told me she used to do a lot of riding, but since she and her father came to Hampstead she's hardly been in the saddle at all.'

'You think it's a possibility?' Grant sounded doubtful. 'She's only been here a few days. And that's supposing she's here at all.'

'It's worth trying, isn't it?'

'Anything's worth trying.'

They left the Maestro at the side of the road and walked over to the gate. It had an iron catch, and Grant released the catch and the gate opened with a squeal of protest from unoiled hinges. There was an odour of hay and stable manure, and ahead of them was a pond with some ducks swimming on it. The pond had a fringe of elder trees and stinging-nettles and cow-parsley, and there was a scum of green weed floating on the surface.

They heard a voice, very loud, very upper class. 'Are you people looking for someone?'

A woman had appeared from a doorway on the left. She was tall and stringy and was dressed in jodhpurs and a yellow jumper.

'As a matter of fact we are,' Grant said.

'Perhaps I can help you. I'm Mrs Green.'

'My name is Grant. This is Miss Jones.' He produced the photograph. 'I wonder whether you've seen this girl anywhere around.'

Mrs Green took one glance at the photograph. 'Oh, you mean Miss Harris. Yes, of course. Only recently come here, you know. Rides very well. Not here today, though.'

'Do you know where she's living?'

'Certainly.' Mrs Green seemed about to tell them but became suddenly wary. 'I don't know whether I ought to give that information. Why do you want to find her?'

'It's all right, you know,' Cynara said. 'I'm a friend of Margarita's. We happened to be in the area and thought we'd look her up; but all I could remember was the name of the village. We've been asking around but nobody seems to have heard of her.'

'They're a dozy lot,' Mrs Green said. She gave Cynara a hard look and seemed to come to the conclusion that she could be trusted. 'Your friend is living in a cottage called Swallows. It's pretty isolated. You get to it down a lane which leads nowhere and you could hunt for donkey's years if you didn't know where it was.'

She went on to give minute directions

concerning the way to get to Swallows. They thanked her and walked back to the car. Some young girls on ponies were just returning to the stables, and Grant held the gate open for them. Then he got into the Maestro, turned it and went in search of the cottage.

*   *   *

The lane was narrow and winding, and it had never been tarred. There were potholes and loose stones, and in places grass was growing on it. There were ditches on each side, but these had become overgrown with brambles and quickthorn and a great variety of weeds which were thriving in blessed freedom from killing sprays. At decent intervals along the lane were cottages, some in pairs, some single, but these dwindled away as they went deeper into the wilderness. They came to a humpbacked bridge over a sluggish stream, and after another hundred yards or so the lane finally gave up the struggle and merged with the brambles and the quickthorn, and that was that.

Swallows was on the left-hand side. The lane just managed to reach it, but it was at the last gasp. The cottage stood a dozen yards back from the lane, and there were three old railway sleepers serving as a footbridge over what had once been the ditch but was now almost filled in. There was a garden of sorts, but it looked as though somebody had done a quick job on it with a motor-scythe and a rotary tiller, and already the weeds were springing up to choke the shrubs that had been planted.

The cottage itself was built of clay and plastered on the outside, and the walls were tarred to a height of about three feet. The roof was tiled and was very steep, indicating that it had probably been thatched originally. There were dormer windows in the upper rooms and the casements were made of iron. There was a lean-to at one end, and the whole place had been given a recent coat of paint, probably to make it more presentable as a holiday home. The name Swallows was on one of those fancy boards sliced from the trunk of a tree and with the bark still on. It was hanging by plastic chains from a small gibbet and it looked all wrong somehow; mock rustic.

Grant and Cynara crossed the sleeper bridge and walked up to the front door. There was no bell-push but there was an iron knocker with which Grant gave a couple of raps. Nothing happened; there was not a sound inside the cottage. Behind it a thicket of alders and willows encroached to within ten yards of the building and stole much of the light. Grant used the knocker again, with no better result.

'So she's out,' Cynara said. 'It's hardly surprising. Who would want to stick in a place like this all alone?'

'It's not exactly a cheerful spot, is it. I wouldn't want all those damned trees on my doorstep. Can you imagine what it would be like in winter?'

'Now what do we do? Stick around until she comes back or go away and return later?'

'I think we'd better stay for a while. She may not have gone far.'

They did some reconnoitring round the cottage. There was nothing of any great interest. They peeped in at the windows, and what they could see of the interior had a cosy enough look about it. One room had an open fireplace and a couple of armchairs and a sofa with loose covers in a kind of floral design. In what appeared to be the kitchen there was a sink with a pump on one side of it and a Calor gas cooker.

'No electricity and no mains water apparently,' Grant said. 'Primitive.'

They were at the back of the cottage when they heard a car coming down the lane, and they hurried round to the front. The car had arrived when they reached the footbridge; it was a blue Mini and there was a girl at the wheel. Grant was ahead of Cynara and he saw that the girl was turning the car as quickly as she could, as though to make a rapid retreat. He caught a glimpse of her face and thought she looked scared.

Even for a Mini there was not much room for the manoeuvre in the narrow lane, and she

111

backed a little too far and got the two rear wheels stuck in one of the dry ditches. The front wheels began to spin and they were not getting enough grip to haul the car out. She must have realised she was not going to make it, for she stopped the engine and opened the door.

Grant reached the car as she was getting out. He said: 'You didn't do that very well, did you?' And then he cut the chatter because he found himself staring into the muzzle of a small automatic pistol which the girl was pointing at him.

It looked like one of the little Berettas, the .22 Plinker model perhaps. People would tell you that something that size was not a real man-stopper, but it stopped Grant; the girl had her finger on the trigger and he had no desire to take even a twenty-two slug in the pit of his stomach, or any other part of his body if it came to that. And he very much hoped it would not come to that.

'Get out of my way,' the girl said; and her hand was shaking a bit and her voice was not completely under control; which seemed to indicate rather less confidence than she was trying to show. 'Don't touch me.'

'I'm not going to touch you,' Grant said; and he made no move with the hands, because this was obviously a pretty touchy young lady, and the less cause he gave her for nervousness the better it might be for all concerned.

And then he heard Cynara's voice behind him. 'Why, Margarita, what are you doing? You're not going to shoot Sam, are you? He's quite harmless, you know.'

The girl, who still had only one leg out of the car, looked past Grant and must have seen Cynara for the first time clearly enough to recognise her. She lowered the gun, and Grant was able to breathe more freely. Cynara came up and pushed him out of the way.

'It's all right,' she said. 'He's a friend.'

Margarita got fully out of the Mini. She seemed embarrassed by the pistol in her hand and she slipped the safety-catch on and stowed it away in her handbag, which had been lying on the seat of the car.

'Do you always carry a gun?' Cynara asked.

'No, no. It's just that—well, I thought it was that other man. I can see it's not now. And it's a different car. I didn't realise. I just didn't stop to think. I suppose I panicked. It was silly.'

'What other man? Has somebody else been here?'

'Yes, earlier. I saw him snooping round when I looked out of the window. And then he came to the door.'

'What did he want?'

'He said he was a council official and that he was checking up on the occupants of all the houses in the area. But I'm sure he was lying. He didn't show any credentials and he wasn't

113

even writing anything down. He asked if there was anyone else in the house?'

'And you said there wasn't?'

'Yes. I said it without thinking.'

'Then what did he do?'

'He gave a kind of smirk and thanked me for my co-operation and went away.'

'What did this man look like?' Grant asked.

'He was fat and he had a spotty face.'

'Sounds like a man I know. And you think I look like that?'

It brought a slightly apologetic smile to her face. 'No, not at all. I didn't really look. I'm sorry.'

'No harm done. But I'm glad you didn't shoot me. Would you have done it if I'd made a false move?'

She answered frankly: 'I don't know. Perhaps I would, perhaps I wouldn't. I just don't know.'

Grant looked at the Mini. 'I suppose you were going to turn round and drive away when you saw my car?'

'Yes.'

'You made a bit of a mess of it, didn't you? Perhaps if Cynara and I were to give a push you could get it out.'

They managed it without much trouble; with two shoulders giving a heave at the back, the front wheels got a grip and the rear wheels came out of the shallow dry ditch.

Margarita thanked them for their help.

'You'd better come indoors. I still don't know why you're here or how you found me.'

They went back to the cottage, and this time she fished a key out of the handbag instead of the gun. She unlocked the door, and they stepped straight into the room where the loose-covered chairs and sofa were.

'Please sit down,' Margarita said. 'I think it's time for you to start explaining. Why are you here?'

'I think you may have some explaining to do, too,' Cynara told her. 'But the answer to your question is simple: Edgar.'

It seemed to startle her. 'What about Edgar?'

'You've got him worried, that's what.'

'But there's no need for him to be worried about me.'

'No need! When you break an appointment and suddenly disappear and he can't find out where you are. How can you expect him not to be worried? He's in love with you, for God's sake. And he thinks you're in love with him. Are you?'

Margarita coloured slightly. 'Yes, I am.'

'Then why run away like this?'

'I can't tell you.'

'No? Do you know what he thinks? He thinks your father sent you away because of him.'

'Because of Edgar?'

'Yes. He thinks your old man doesn't

approve of your getting involved with him, so he packed you off somewhere to keep the two of you apart.'

'But that's ridiculous. It isn't the reason at all. My father quite likes Edgar. He doesn't mind my seeing him a bit.'

'Well, I'm sure it'll make him very happy to hear that. But you still haven't given the real reason why you were sent down here all of a sudden. You were sent, weren't you? So why?'

Margarita was silent.

Grant said: 'I never did think it had anything to do with Edgar. It's something far bigger than that, isn't it? Political maybe.'

She glanced at him sharply. 'Political?'

'It has to do with the politics of your country, doesn't it?'

'What do you know about that?'

'I think your father's name was previously not Harris but Harrera. I think he was thrown out of office as president by a military coup.'

She did not deny it. Perhaps she thought it would have been pointless to do so.

'What happened to make it necessary for you to leave London and hide yourself down here?' Cynara asked. 'You can tell us. We may be able to help.'

Margarita shook her head. 'I don't think you can, but I'll tell you anyway; I don't see that there's any harm in it now. Ever since the coup my father has believed his life to be in danger. A week or two ago some

116

compromising material came into his hands which he saw could give him a hold on the leader of the junta, General Alvarez. It seemed like a safeguard, but things have turned out not quite as he expected. A man named Velasco, a captain in the army and a nephew of Alvarez, came to see him. He offered to buy the material, and when my father refused to part with it he used threats. From what he said my father concluded that he and another man named Guayama would try to kidnap me and bring pressure to bear in that way.'

'So he sent you here to keep you out of harm.'

'Yes. I wanted to tell Edgar, but he was against it. He said nobody must know and that I must not even write a letter from here. What I don't understand is how you found me.'

'By guess and luck. I remembered you saying something about this cottage, and with a bit of memory jogging I came up with the name of the village.'

'Your father told us you were on the Continent and there was no way of getting in touch with you,' Grant said.

'You've been to see him?'

'Yes. That was the first thing we did.'

'But you didn't believe him?'

'No. He said you'd been planning it for some time and it seemed to us unlikely that you would have said nothing to Edgar.'

She was silent, apparently thinking over what she had heard. Then she said: 'What do you propose doing now that you've found me?'

'The idea was to report back to Edgar. He's the one who started the hunt.'

'And are you going to do that?'

'For the present I think not.'

Cynara glanced at him with a lift of the eyebrows. 'Why not?'

'The situation is somewhat altered, don't you see?'

'In what way?'

'Freddy Granger has stepped into the picture.'

'Who is Freddy Granger?' Margarita asked.

'The fat man with the spots. We saw him in the village and I recognised him. He's a private detective and my guess is he's working for your two men, Velasco and Guayama.'

'How do you know he's a private detective?'

'I happen to be in the same line of business.'

'Oh,' she said; and she gave him a hard look and he wondered whether she was thinking of asking him to leave the room now that she knew what he did for a living. 'Are you saying Edgar employed you to find me?'

'Don't hold it against him. He was worried sick about you.'

'And anyway,' Cynara said, 'you can't really say he's employing Sam because he'd have to go to Mr Peking to do that. Actually Sam is on holiday.'

'Who is Mr Peking?' Margarita asked.

'He's my boss,' Grant said. 'But let's not bring him into it. It's complicated enough already. I think you ought to clear out.'

'Clear out!'

'Leave this place. If Freddy Granger really is working for the other two—and who else would he be working for?—he'll be getting in touch with them pretty soon, even if he hasn't done so already. And then they'll be paying you a visit before long. You're not safe here any more.'

She looked worried. 'But where can I go? It would be no use going back to Hampstead.'

'I've got an idea,' Cynara said. 'Why don't you move in with us for the time being?'

'With you?'

'Yes, Sam and me, at his flat. We're living together now. Didn't you know?'

'How could she have known?' Grant said. 'You only moved in the evening before last.'

'Only as long as that! It seems ages.' She was teasing him and there was laughter in her eyes.

'Anyway, it's not on,' he said. 'There's only one bedroom.'

'Oh, I'm sure we can work things out. In an emergency like this something has to give.'

Grant reflected that he might be the something. He had a nasty feeling that he might find himself sleeping on the sofa in the living-room while the girls shared the bed. It

119

would not be the first time that sort of thing had happened. And it was certainly not the way he had planned to spend his holiday.

But Margarita seemed to have reservations regarding the proposal. 'I don't know. It hardly seems—'

'Don't raise objections,' Cynara said. 'You can't stay here with those two men plotting to kidnap you. You've got to go somewhere. And it would be only temporary.'

Margarita looked at Grant. 'You're not happy with the idea, are you? And it is your flat.'

He felt himself being driven into a corner. And the only thing he could say was: 'Oh, it'll be all right for a few days. Until we can fix up something better.'

'Well,' she said, 'let's have lunch and I'll think about it.'

'That sounds like a good idea,' Cynara said. 'I'm starving. We had an early breakfast. Have you got enough food?'

'If you don't mind things out of cans.'

'Not a bit.'

When they were eating the things out of cans Grant asked Margarita where she had got the gun.

'Oh,' she said, 'my father gave it to me.'

'And you know how to use it?'

'In my country,' she said, 'everybody knows how to use a gun.'

'That's probably the trouble with it,' Grant

120

said. 'In this country it's illegal to possess a firearm without a permit. Have you got one?'

'Don't harry the poor girl,' Cynara said. 'You sound like a policeman.'

Margarita said nothing. Grant saw that he was not going to get an answer. He guessed she had no permit for the Beretta, but it was not his business.

When they had finished lunch Margarita said she had thought things over and come to the conclusion that she would stay one more night in the cottage and maybe drive up to London in the morning. Grant had a feeling that she could not make up her mind what to do and was postponing making a definite decision.

'Then we'll stay here with you,' Cynara said.

'Oh, there's no need for you to do that.'

'No need! Of course there is. Do you think we're going to leave you here by yourself? With those beastly men looking for you. We couldn't do it, could we, Sam?'

She was not really asking his opinion but demanding support for hers. 'Well,' he said, 'it's up to Margarita. Perhaps it wouldn't be convenient.'

'Damn convenience. There's more at stake than that. Anyway, I bet it wouldn't be inconvenient at all. How many bedrooms are there, Margarita?'

'Two, but—'

'There you are, Sam; two bedrooms. That's

twice as many as there are in your poky little flat.'

'You are very welcome to stay,' Margarita said. 'But please don't feel that you have to.'

'But you really do want us to, don't you?'

She admitted it. 'Yes, I do.'

'That's settled then.'

Grant shrugged, resigned to the arrangement. It looked as though Cynara had taken over the planning. He just hoped it would all work out satisfactorily.

There was still half the day left and it was his suggestion that they should drive out to the coast; there seemed to be no point in hanging around in the cottage. There were no objections from the girls, and he drove the Maestro with Cynara sitting beside him and Margarita in the back. They left the Mini in the lane with the doors locked, and they locked the cottage, too.

It was less than twenty miles to Great Yarmouth, and they arrived at about half-past three. Grant found a parking place for the car, and then they mingled with the crowds of holidaymakers like any ordinary trippers. Grant was surprised to see how much Margarita seemed to be enjoying it all. It was the first time she had ever visited an English seaside resort and she was loving the novelty of it. For the moment she seemed to have forgotten the threat that hung over her, but on the way back to Wendleham in the evening she became silent and Grant guessed that it was weighing on her mind again.

It was weighing on his mind, too. He wondered whether anyone had turned up at the cottage during their absence, because if Freddy Granger had been in touch with his clients on the telephone it would not have taken them long to drive down from London and rendezvous with him at the village. It was still largely supposition, of course, that he was indeed working for Velasco and Guayama, but it was so strong a supposition that Grant himself had already accepted it as hard fact. It was for this reason that when he took the Maestro into the lane in the gathering darkness of the late evening he was on the alert for any hint of danger.

He drove at reduced speed past the other cottages and had left the last of them a quarter of a mile behind when he came to the humpbacked bridge. He drove even more slowly over the bridge and saw the final hundred yards or so of road illuminated by the headlamps. He could see the Mini standing where they had left it, and if there had been any other car there as well he would have turned the Maestro and driven away fast. But there was no other car and he felt a sense of relief and relaxed a little.

Cynara gave a faint sigh, and he guessed that she had been a bit tensed up too. 'Well,' she said, 'it looks like no visitors.'

'They could have been and gone,' Grant said. He was still being cautious. He drew the Maestro to a halt beside the Mini.

'Anyway, there's no one around,' Cynara said. 'And that's the main thing.'

None of them had got out of the car, though Grant had stopped the engine and switched off the lights. He glanced towards the cottage. The walls, pale above the black tar, had a ghostly look against the dark background of the trees. There was no light showing in any of the windows and there was no sound except for the hooting of an owl intent upon its own nocturnal business.

'I suppose we're not intending to sit out here all night,' Cynara said. 'Come along.'

She opened the door and got out of the car. Margarita and Grant followed her example. Grant locked the car and Margarita led the way across the sleeper bridge, treading carefully in the darkness. She came to the door of the cottage, unlocked it and went inside. Grant was the last to go in and he closed the door behind him. The interior of the cottage was in complete darkness and he could hear Margarita groping around in the room.

'I'm looking for the matches,' she said.

'Ah, the delights of the simple life,' Cynara remarked. 'Why didn't somebody think to bring a torch from the car?'

And then one of the girls gave a shriek, though Grant could not be sure which of them it was, and he heard a man laugh.

A light came on suddenly, and Grant saw that it was a fluorescent battery lamp perched on the mantelpiece above the fireplace. Standing on one side of it was a man in a leather jacket and brown trousers. Sitting in one of the armchairs and looking very much at his ease was another man dressed in a double-breasted navy blue blazer, pale grey trousers and suede shoes. All very natty.

The man in the chair was holding a nine millimetre Luger self-loading pistol in his right hand. He was smiling.

CHAPTER TEN

SOME HOLIDAY

It was the man in the leather jacket who had laughed and Margarita who had uttered the shriek. In searching for the box of matches on the mantelpiece her fingers had touched the man and she had recoiled in shock.

'Welcome home,' the man in the armchair said. 'We have been expecting you hourly, but no doubt you have been enjoying yourselves. Now please do nothing stupid, for I assure you this weapon is loaded and I would not hesitate to use it.' He spoke to the man in the leather jacket. 'Diego, see if they are armed.'

125

The man obeyed his instructions with efficiency but no delicacy; he handled the girls with evident enjoyment, leering at them as he did so. He was broad-shouldered and barrel-chested, but not tall. His curling black hair was closely trimmed and his face was scarred. He had a thick moustache and a wide, cruel mouth.

Grant had no difficulty in guessing that he was Guayama and that the man with the pistol was Velasco; it was questionable just which was the more dangerous of the two, the brutal ugly sergeant or the smooth handsome captain. He would have felt safer with a pair of cobras in the room.

'You are probably wondering how we got in,' Velasco said. 'To ease your curiosity I will tell you; it was through a window at the back. It had not been fastened. Very careless.'

Grant supposed they had concealed their car somewhere; it was unlikely that they had walked; neither of them looked the kind of man who would do much walking from choice.

Guayama reported that there were no hidden weapons. Grant could see Margarita's handbag on a side-table to the left of the fireplace where she had dumped it when searching for the matches. He had no doubt that the Beretta was still in it and he hoped she would do nothing reckless, but he was not counting on it.

'Good,' Velasco said. 'Now we can relax. It

surprises you perhaps, Señorita Harrera, to find us here. You cannot understand how we could have traced you to this hiding-place where the ex-Presidente so carefully sent you for safety.'

'Don't kid yourself,' Grant said. 'She knows perfectly well how you did it. You hired that bastard Granger to trace her for you. When he had done that he rang you up and arranged for you to meet him in the village. Then he showed you where this place was and made himself scarce, because he wouldn't want to be mixed up in anything you're planning to do. He may be a crook but he's a careful crook; he likes to keep his nose at least partly clean.'

Velasco smiled. 'Ah, of course, I had forgotten that you are acquainted with Mr Granger. He told me about you. Mr Grant, isn't it? And this other young lady is your fiancée? How charming. But you really should not have interfered in this business which has nothing whatever to do with you. You have complicated matters, but only slightly. We shall still carry out the operation as we intended. In fact, this cottage will make a most convenient base. It will spare us the necessity of finding some alternative accommodation.'

'What you are saying,' Grant said, 'is that you intend to keep us all here as prisoners while you try to force Mr Harrera to do what you want him to do. Is that it?'

'You are very quick to get the hang of

127

things. Obviously we could not allow you and your fiancée—if she is your fiancée—to go around telling people what we are doing; it might attract unwelcome attention. Later, when this affair is concluded satisfactorily, you will be permitted to leave, but not before.'

'And Miss Harrera?'

'She, too, of course.'

'Unharmed?'

'Now who,' Velasco said, 'is talking about harm? Have I said anything about harming anyone?'

'Perhaps it isn't necessary to say it.'

Margarita had been standing close to the mantelpiece on the opposite side of the fireplace to Guayama. Behind her was the small side-table with the handbag lying on it. Out of the corner of his eye Grant saw her put her hands behind her back and reach for the bag. No one else was watching her and he guessed what she intended doing. It was crazy and he wanted to shout her to stop it right there, but he said nothing. A moment later she had the bag open and the Beretta was in her hand.

She was quick; there was no doubt about that. She slipped the safety-catch off and there must already have been a round in the chamber because she just pointed the weapon at Velasco and pressed the trigger, and it fired.

But she had been just a little too quick; she had not given herself time to take careful aim, and though the distance was small the bullet missed Velasco by a whisker and went into the upholstery of the chair. But it was a damned close thing and it gave him a shock. He let out a yelp and jerked away to his left as if he had been stung by a hornet.

Guayama made a kind of grunting sound. He took one step across the fireplace and hit Margarita on the side of the face with the back of his hand before she could fire again. The blow almost lifted her off her feet; it slammed her against the wall and from there she fell to the floor, too dazed to get up immediately. Guayama grabbed the Beretta.

As soon as Margarita fired the gun and missed Velasco, Grant stepped forward and kicked the Luger out of his hand. It skittered along the floor and he gave Velasco a pile-driver in the stomach to keep him occupied and went for the gun. He had his fingers on it when he heard Cynara scream a warning.

'Look out, Sam! Look out!'

But it was too late to do any looking out because Guayama was already on him; and he was never sure whether Guayama hit him with the Beretta or just his iron-hard fist; but whichever it was, it was effective. It doused the lights as far as he was concerned.

*   *   *

When he came to he was in complete darkness

129

and there was an unpleasant odour in his nostrils which he finally concluded was coming from the damp brick floor on which he was lying. His head and neck were aching, and at first he was so disorientated that he had difficulty in remembering just what had happened. Then it all came back to him and he was not sure it might not have been a deal more pleasing if it had not.

He wished Margarita had never taken it into her head to go for the Beretta; or if she had to do it he wished she had plugged Velasco dead centre, because then he might have been able to handle Guayama. He would not have made any bets on it, because Guayama looked like one hell of a big handful, but there would have been a chance. Now it looked as though they had slung him in some kind of shed and probably locked him in; and his guess was that he was in the lean-to on the end of the cottage.

He sat up, and his head swam and he felt sick. He was not sure whether he felt as sick as a dog because no dog had ever told him how sick it felt, but he really did feel sick. He took some deep breaths of the somewhat dank air, and after a while he felt rather better and managed to get on to his feet.

After this he began to reconnoitre his prison, and it really was a prison, for he came to a door with a latch, and though he lifted the latch the door refused to budge. There seemed to be no lock on it, so he concluded that there was either a bolt or a hasp and staple on the outside which was fastened with a padlock or simply an iron pin. He continued his navigation of the prison, and on one side the roof was no more than a foot or so above his head, which seemed to prove that it was indeed the lean-to. On the opposite side was another door which had to give access to the kitchen, but that was fastened securely also. He listened but could hear no sound on the other side.

In one corner he discovered what he divined to be an old-fashioned copper bricked into the angle of the walls and with a fire-hole under it. He gathered from this that the lean-to had in the past been used as a wash-house. All this information that he was soaking up was doing him no good at all; he was still a prisoner. There ought to have been a window, but he could not find one; which was odd, to say the least.

He could not see to read his watch, but he reckoned the time had to be well past eleven and he could have used some sleep. But there was nothing to lie on except the hard brick floor, and he doubted whether it would have been at all easy to get the sandman to pay a call in such uncomfortable conditions. And this was supposed to be his holiday, damn it. Some holiday!

When he had groped around some more he found what felt like a large cardboard carton.

He tore it down the edges and folded it flat so that he could use it as a kind of cushion, and then he sat on this cardboard sandwich with his back supported by one of the walls. It was far from comfortable, but in spite of this he began to nod after a while, and he might even have snatched a little sleep if there had not been a sudden interruption.

It was a girl's scream; and not just one but a succession of them going on and on. The sound came to him somewhat muffled by the intervening doors, but it was enough to bring him fully awake, and he thought he had never heard such an expression of agony in a human voice. He knew that it was one of the girls, but which? And what in hell were they doing to her? Torture? Rape? There was no way of telling. The only certainty was that they were doing something, and it had to be bad to produce such an outburst of screaming.

The bastards! He went to the door separating the lean-to from the rest of the cottage and made a frenzied attempt to break it down; but the only result of his efforts was a bruised shoulder and a sense of impotence and utter frustration.

And gradually the screaming ebbed away, sinking to a kind of sobbing note which faded into inaudibility. Tears might now be flowing, but he could not see the teardrops and he could not hear the weeping; it was all up to his imagination now, and that was vivid enough and sombre enough to prevent any further essays at sleeping. He was filled with a sullen anger and a burning desire for revenge, and he could do nothing but wait for the weary hours to pass.

*   *   *

It began to get light very early. By four o'clock he was able to make out the time by his watch and he knew why there was no window: the light came in by way of some glass tiles in the roof. There was no ceiling and he could see the rafters and the slats with the tiles lying on them. He now discovered also that the outer door was in two halves like that of a stable, so that the upper half might be opened independently of the lower to allow light and air to come in. Unfortunately, at the present moment neither half could be opened because they were both securely fastened on the outside.

After another hour had passed the interior of the lean-to was clearly revealed by the light coming through the glass tiles. The walls were whitewashed and the place was practically bare apart from the flattened cardboard carton. There was a wealth of cobweb hanging from the rafters and the brick floor had been worn by years and possibly centuries of use to a state of extreme unevenness. He saw that he had been correct in identifying the copper in one corner, and there was a worm-eaten wooden lid covering the top of it. Nowhere could he see anything that might have been used as a lever or battering-ram to force open the door. He tried breaking up the lid of the copper for possible use as a club, but it practically fell to pieces in his hands because of the ravages of woodworm, and it was useless for his purpose.

It was nearly eight o'clock before anyone looked in on him, though he had heard sounds of movement in the cottage and had shouted and hammered on the inner door with his fists and feet. He had long since abandoned this futile exercise when the door opened and Guayama appeared.

Guayama was carrying a plate with some biscuits and slices of luncheon meat on it and a mug of coffee. He set the plate and the mug down on the floor and grinned at the prisoner.

'You want eat?' He spoke English with an atrocious accent and faint regard for syntax.

'You bastard,' Grant said. 'What were you doing to those girls last night?'

Guayama grinned again, as though the memory was pleasing to him, and Grant felt a mad impulse to rush at the man and start hitting him. But it would have served no useful purpose. Even if he had managed to overpower this animal, which would not have been an easy task even if possible at all, there would still have been Velasco with the Luger.

'One girl,' Guayama said. 'Just one girl.'

'Which one, damn you?'

'You guess.'

'Tell me.'

Guayama stood in the doorway, almost filling it with his wide body. 'Both damn pretty girls. One last night, maybe other one tonight. Have good time, huh?' He was enjoying himself, goading his prisoner, taunting him, tormenting him. And loving it.

Grant controlled himself with difficulty. He saw that he would get no straight answer from Guayama on that subject. He said: 'How long are you going to keep me in here?'

Guayama made a gesture with his hands. 'Two day, three day. Why you ask? Not happy here? Not sleep good?'

'I didn't sleep at all.'

'Too bad,' Guayama said. He went away, closing and bolting the door behind him.

There was no knife and no fork with the food. Grant ate it and drank the coffee. Later he heard a car start up and drive away. He guessed it was the one that had been hidden. He wondered who had left in it; Velasco or Guayama or maybe both? He would have said that it was Velasco and that Guayama had been left behind to guard the captives. He had confirmation of this when Guayama put in a second appearance at one o'clock to bring him another meal. This time it was stew in a bowl and more biscuits. A plastic spoon was provided and there was also a glass of water. It

135

was scarcely haute cuisine but perhaps he should have felt himself lucky to get anything at all; he might have been left to starve.

'Where's Velasco gone?' he asked.

'No questions,' Guayama said, 'no lies.'

Grant wanted to ask whether the girls were well, but he would probably have got the same answer to that, so he held his tongue.

'You okay?' Guayama asked.

'Your concern for my health touches me,' Grant said. 'Do you think I might go to the lavatory?'

'Huh?'

Grant said it again in sign language.

Guayama laughed. 'Plenty room here.' He picked up the breakfast plate and the mug and went away.

It was a warm day. In the wash-house it had become quite hot. From the other part of the cottage there came scarcely a sound. Grant wondered what the girls were doing. He wondered whether they had been locked away, together or separately. Possibly they were in one of the bedrooms. He thought again of that screaming in the night. There had been no more of that, thank God. Yet.

Velasco had not yet returned. What errand had taken him away from the cottage? Had he gone up to London to see Harrera? Probably. And if so, what would Harrera's reaction be? Would he be stubborn? Margarita had not said what the compromising material in his

136

possession was, but perhaps she herself did not know. It had to be something pretty strong to make Alvarez send Velasco to get possession of it. And Harrera would certainly be reluctant to part with it if it was the only means of safeguarding his life. Yet could he hold out, knowing that his daughter was in the hands of such men as Velasco and Guayama?

Grant turned his mind to the problem of escaping from the wash-house. Only by getting free himself could he hope to do anything for Margarita and Cynara. But the prison seemed to be strong; the walls were thick and to tunnel under them without tools would have been a process so slow and difficult that it was not worth consideration. Besides which, any hole and the material taken from it would have been seen by Guayama as soon as he brought another meal.

So was there some other way? Some means by which he could deal with Guayama before Velasco returned. If he intended doing anything in that line it had better be done as soon as Guayama paid him another visit, for there was no telling when the other man would be back. He wondered when the next meal would be served. The nature of the food seemed to indicate that Guayama was not letting either of the girls into the kitchen but was doing the catering himself with the aid of a tin-opener. Lunch had been at one o'clock, but it was anybody's guess at what time he would serve tea, or even whether he would bother to serve it at all.

Grant again searched for some kind of weapon. The thought came to him that if he could dig up one of the bricks from the floor he might use it as a bludgeon; but none of them appeared to be loose and he could not budge them with his fingers. He searched his pockets for some implement to use and found a nail-file. With this thin tool he began to pick away at the crevice between two of the bricks, gradually working his way round one of them and digging out the hard-packed earth that had become jammed into this narrow space. After nearly an hour of this tedious work he could still not shift the brick, but he persevered and at last it began to loosen. The file broke when he tried to use it as a lever, but he had more success with a two-penny coin and finally lifted the brick out of its resting-place.

He now had his bludgeon. He weighed the brick in his hand, and he thought it would do the job. He took the cardboard cushion to the door and sat down on it to wait with the brick on the floor beside him, listening for the sound of Guayama's approach.

CHAPTER ELEVEN

PROMOTION ASSURED

After leaving the cottage Velasco drove himself back to London in his rented Vauxhall Cavalier. He arrived at his hotel a few minutes after midday and went to the room which he had not used the previous night. He was carrying in his hand a white polythene bag and with him he also had a paper bag containing a small cardboard box, some tissue-paper and a reel of Scotch tape which he had bought at a stationer's shop in Holborn.

For a time in his room he was busy with the materials he had brought in. When he had finished his task he rang down to the reception-desk and made a request. The desk-clerk was only too happy to oblige; it was the kind of hotel that prided itself on the service it provided for its guests.

'I will send someone to your room in five minutes, sir.'

Velasco thanked him and replaced the telephone. Five minutes later precisely there came a discreet tap on the door, and Velasco admitted to the room a pale young man in a grey suit.

'You are the special messenger?'

The pale young man said he was and that he

139

was at Velasco's service.

Velasco handed him the cardboard box, now securely fastened with Scotch tape. 'I want you to deliver this parcel to the address on the box. You will hand it personally to the man named on the address. You do not need to tell him who sent you. When you have done this you will come back to me here and report that the delivery has been made. You understand?'

'Perfectly, sir.'

The pale young man departed, and Velasco went down to the hotel dining-room and ate an excellent lunch. When he had finished his meal he returned to his room. Half an hour later the pale young man again gave his discreet tap on the door and came into the room with the report that his mission had been completed.

'You saw the man to whom the box was addressed?'

'Yes, sir.'

'Describe him to me.'

The pale young man gave a brief description which was entirely satisfactory.

'How did his manner strike you?'

'He seemed nervous, ill-at-ease, I would have said. And he did not seem well.'

'Thank you,' Velasco said. He gave the pale young man a suitable reward and closed the door behind him when he left the room.

*   *   *

140

Harrera was in his study when Mrs Higgs ushered the pale young man into his presence. At a signal from her employer she left the room and closed the door.

'You have something for me, I believe,' Harrera said.

'Yes, sir. This.' The pale young man handed the cardboard box to him. 'I was instructed to hand it only to you in person, Mr Harris.'

Harrera could not control a slight trembling in the hands as he took the box. He had a sense of foreboding that made him feel quite faint.

'Who sent this?'

'My instructions were that it would not be necessary to tell you that.'

'I see. Was there any message?'

'No message, sir.'

'Very well, thank you.'

When the pale young man had gone Harrera took the box to the writing-table by the window and set it down. He felt compelled to sit down because there was a weakness in his legs, and for several minutes he did nothing but sit there and stare fixedly at the box.

At last he screwed up his courage, took a sharp paper-knife in his hand and cut the Scotch tape. When he removed the lid from the box he saw that there was something inside it wrapped in tissue-paper. Lying on top of the wrapping was a slip of writing-paper with a few words inscribed on it in black ink. He picked up the paper and read the message.

'You will receive a telephone call at three o'clock.'

There was no signature, but none was required. He knew who had sent the message and he laid the paper on the desk and stared at the package in the box, guessing at what it might contain and dreading to take away the wrapping and have his fears confirmed.

But it had to be done; he could not simply replace the lid and throw the box away; that was quite out of the question. So finally, with shaking fingers, he lifted out the package, set it down on the table and opened up the wrapping.

Premonition and guessing could not lessen the shock at seeing what was revealed. He gave a cry as of physical pain and shrank back in his chair, wanting to draw his gaze away yet unable to do so, forced against his will to continue staring at the object in front of him.

It lay in its nest of tissue-paper like a pink sea-shell, small and delicate and exquisite, the traces of dried blood bearing mute evidence of the savagery with which it had been sliced from the head to which it had been attached.

'No!' Harrera muttered. 'Oh, no, no!'

The object blurred before his eyes. He did not doubt, could not doubt, that he was looking at one of his daughter's ears. So they had found her; in spite of his precautions they

142

had found her. And they had sent this part of her as a warning, not bothering to discover whether the mere fact of knowing that she was in their hands would have been sufficient to persuade him to do what they desired. The cold-blooded sadism of it appalled him; and yet he had no right to be surprised; in the country from which he had fled worse atrocities happened daily, were commonplace. And these two men had done the vilest things to their fellow human beings without compunction or remorse. To them the severing of the ear of a beautiful young girl would count as nothing.

He sat for some considerable time without moving; then with a shudder he put the ear back in the cardboard box and replaced the lid.

*   *   *

After the departure of the pale young man Velasco smoked a cigarette, glanced through the pages of a glossy magazine, watched a little television and generally killed time until three o'clock. Then he put through an outside telephone call.

Harrera answered the call at once. Velasco could imagine him sitting at his desk and waiting for the bell to ring. There was a hint of tension in his voice as he spoke.

'Well, hello, Mr Harris,' Velasco said,

taunting his victim with the assumed surname. 'I don't imagine there is any need to tell you who this is.'

'No,' Harrera said, 'there is no need at all.'

'You received my little present?'

'You know I did.'

'In case you may be thinking it could be a hoax, not the genuine article, you know, I will just mention the name of an English village—Wendleham. Curious name, that. And a cottage called Swallows at the end of a rough lane; all rather primitive. Need I say more?'

'No.'

'Good. One needs to be wary of saying too much on the telephone. Am I to take it that you now agree to co-operate?'

'I am forced to do so.'

'That is wise. I will call on you tomorrow at this time. Please have the material ready.'

He did not wait for Harrera to say anything else. He rang off and lit another cigarette. He poured himself a glass of whisky and sat in an armchair feeling contented with the way things were going. He did not doubt that Harrera would have the photographs ready to hand over when he called the next day; it was amazing how persuasive a small intrinsically worthless article like a girl's ear could be when delivered to the girl's loving father. It had been best to do it that way; it saved a lot of argument and the entire business would be concluded with admirable promptness.

Velasco smiled as he watched the smoke drifting away from his cigarette. Uncle Bernardo would be pleased with the results. And generous.

That evening he went out on the town and enjoyed himself greatly in the company of an attractive and obliging young female named Gloria who had been supplied by an agency. So obliging was Gloria in fact that she agreed to stay with him for the rest of the night. She was still around in the morning but he got rid of her smartly enough then because he had business to attend to and she had no part to play in that business.

At three o'clock in the afternoon he drove the Cavalier up the drive to the house in Hampstead and rang the bell. Mrs Higgs, who answered the door, had been expecting him, and she showed him into the same room as before, where Harrera was waiting.

'Good afternoon,' Velasco said. 'You see that I am a punctual man.'

Harrera did not praise him for his punctuality, nor did he offer to shake hands. Velasco thought that Harrera looked somehow drained. It was probable that he had spent the past twenty-four hours in far less enjoyable fashion than his visitor.

'You are a vile man,' Harrera said. 'But that no doubt is how you were made.'

Velasco laughed contemptuously, but the remark had angered him. 'Let us not waste our breath on vain insults. Have you collected the photographs?'

'I have.'

'Where are they?'

'One moment,' Harrera said. 'If I give them to you, how do I know that you will release my daughter? I will not say unharmed, since you have harmed her terribly already. But what guarantee do I have that you will release her at all?'

'You have my word.'

'And you think I should trust the word of a man like you?'

'You have little choice,' Velasco said. 'Either you give me the photographs in the hope that I will set the girl free or you refuse to give them to me in the certainty that very soon you will receive another small parcel. And after that another and another. But I am sure you are not going to be obstinate. It would not help you, you know.'

Harrera sighed faintly. He opened a drawer in the writing-table and took out a manila folder which he placed on the time-worn mahogany surface.

'This is what you have come for.'

Velasco advanced to the table. 'Show me.'

'You wish to see what you are getting?'

'Naturally. I have to make a check. And to tell the truth, I am rather curious to see what all the fuss has been about.'

'The general did not show you the two

146

photographs I sent him?'

'No.'

'It is understandable, I suppose; though he must have known you would look at these if you ever got hold of them. He has great trust in you.'

'With reason.'

Harrera opened the folder and spread the photographs out on the table. Velasco examined them in silence. Then he laughed.

'Now I can see why Uncle Bernardo is so keen to get his hands on these pictures. Compromising is hardly a strong enough word to describe them. And the lady: I must confess I have never seen her in the state of nature, which I think you will admit has been my loss. Uncle Bernardo is hardly to be blamed for wanting to make love to such a gorgeous creature. But on the same reckoning General Zaragoza would certainly be as mad as a rabid dog if he were ever to see what we have lying here.'

'No doubt.'

'Of course she is wasted on an old gorilla like him, and I can understand why she would go for a man like Uncle Bernardo, who is well enough endowed physically to attract any woman; but she should have known the risk she was taking. Well, no doubt she did and was simply reckless. Women are so wild in matters of the heart. Uncle Bernardo should have known better; he is not a boy. To share a

147

house in the Bahamas with Zaragoza's wife was the height of folly. Truly I would have expected him to have had more sense.'

Harrera stared at Velasco sombrely. 'You appear to treat the matter very light-heartedly. It seems to be a great joke to you.'

Velasco laughed again. 'And so it is; the best joke in the world. How long is it since these photographs were taken? More than a year, I suppose. It must have been before the military coup; he has been too fully occupied with affairs of state since then to spend much time on affairs of an amorous nature. And all that time he and the lady must have been on tenterhooks, waiting for the things to surface. It's as if they've been sitting on a time-bomb, expecting at any moment to be blown sky-high. Unless, of course, they were not aware that the photographs had been taken. It surprises me that the man who took them should have kept them a secret for so long. Why, I wonder?'

'Because he was afraid,' Harrera said.

'He told you that?'

'He did not tell me, but I guessed. He thought he was safe in selling them to me.'

'Did he tell you his name?'

'He said it was Smith. It was a lie, of course.'

'Of course. But one thing is certain; our Mr Smith is no novice with the camera. You have to admire his work.'

'It is not the kind of work for which I have any admiration,' Harrera said with disdain. 'It

148

is disgusting.'

'You condemn it?'

'Yes.'

'And yet you were willing to make use of it.'

'To my shame. I regret it now.'

'Yes, it's recoiled on you, hasn't it?' Velasco began to gather up the prints and put them back in the folder with the negatives. 'I suppose they are all here?'

'Yes.'

'You haven't kept back a spare set of prints to make use of at some future date?'

'No.'

'I hope you are telling the truth—for your sake as well as mine. Because if you are not, if you try to play the same trick again, then I shall come back and deal with the situation. I shall find your charming daughter again, whatever you do to protect her. And next time I may not be so lenient with her.'

'Lenient!' Harrera's voice rose in outrage. 'You hack off her ear and you have the gall to call that leniency?'

'I did not remove the ear. It was Diego who did it.'

'Your personal butcher. Does that make you any the less guilty?'

Velasco snapped his fingers. 'Let us not talk of guilt. The word means nothing to me.' He picked up the folder. 'I will leave you now.'

'And pay nothing for the photographs, of course.' Harrera's tone was bitter. He had lost both the money he had paid to Mendes and the shield which that money had bought. In return he had received nothing but the mutilation of his daughter.

'It is your own fault,' Velasco said. 'You could have been well paid if you had accepted my offer. You chose not to, and the refusal cost me a deal of extra work and some expense. I think I am entitled to take what I have.'

'When will you release Margarita?'

'As soon as I get back to Wendleham. I will take Diego with me and we will probably be out of the country tomorrow. Her friends will be released at the same time.'

'Her friends?'

'Ah, you didn't know? A man called Grant and a young lady named Cynara Jones.'

'So they also found her?'

'Yes. You see how easily it can be done. They gave us a little trouble but we were able to handle it.'

'I do not doubt it,' Harrera said. He looked at Velasco with hatred. 'You handle everything, everything. One day perhaps retribution will catch up with you.'

'Ha!' Velasco said. 'You believe in the theory that justice must finally prevail. You of all men should know better than that. So do not console yourself with the thought that I shall come to a bad end. I know too well how to look after myself. Goodbye, Señor Harrera.

We may meet again, but I doubt it.'

There had been no handshake at meeting and there was none at parting. Velasco left the house and drove away in the Cavalier, well satisfied with the way things had gone. He had carried out his orders with efficiency and success. Now his promotion was assured.

CHAPTER TWELVE

THE JACKPOT

Grant had to wait a considerable time before he heard Guayama pulling back the bolts on the door. He took the brick in his hand, got up quickly and stood at the hinged side of the door, poised to attack the man as soon as he stepped into the wash-house.

The door opened with a squeal of hinges, hiding Grant from the sight of his gaoler. He waited, holding his breath, and the first thing he saw was the tray which Guayama was carrying. The edge of the tray projected about two inches beyond the door and then stopped. Grant realised that Guayama had looked into the wash-house, and not being able to see the prisoner had become suspicious. He heard the man's grating voice.

'Where you hide? You come out now. You show you damn self.'

Grant saw that things were not going according to plan. There was no way he was going to entice Guayama to take those two more steps that would set him up for a crack on the head with the brick. So what to do now? Put the brick down and show himself, hoping that Guayama would not notice it or the hole in the floor from which he had taken it? He was reluctant to abandon his attempt to break out, because time was passing and there might not be another chance.

Guayama spoke again. 'No tricks now. You let me see you damn face. Pronto.'

Grant decided not to wait any longer. He moved swiftly round the edge of the door and took a swing at Guayama with the brick. It might have been a very effective piece of action indeed if Guayama had not moved, but he was already on the alert and his reflexes were in good order. He shifted his head like a boxer avoiding a punch to the chin, and the brick went past it on the left-hand side. Grant's wrist came up hard against Guayama's collar-bone and the jarring impact numbed his hand. The brick slipped from his fingers and sailed on under its own momentum, finally coming to rest under the kitchen table.

The plate and the mug that were on the tray slid off it, spilling their contents and breaking to shards on the floor of the wash-house. Guayama retained his grip on the tray with his right hand and hit Grant with it on the side of the head, knocking him against the door. The door swung further open, and Grant, dazed by the blow, stumbled and fell. Guayama followed up and kicked him in the ribs.

'You think you crack my head, huh? You think you give me hard time? I give you hard time, you goddam sonuvabitch, you.'

He planted another kick on the rib-cage, and it hurt. Grant managed to get a hold on his ankle and tried to upset his balance and bring him to the ground in order to put them on level terms—if you could ever be on level terms when fighting a gorilla. Guayama hit him again with the tray. It was taking an unfair advantage, but he probably thought it was only making up for the brick. He seemed to be highly resentful of that attempt to brain him and was being distinctly vicious in retaliation.

Grant lost his grip on Guayama's ankle and received another kick. He had a feeling that he was not doing too well; he also had a feeling that Guayama was maybe going to kill him; which would be a pretty rotten thing to happen on holiday. Not that it would have been at all pleasant even if he had been on normal Peking Agency business; there was no way being killed by this bastard was going to be the most delightful experience in the world, whatever the circumstances. But somehow it seemed worse on holiday because you expected better things when you were taking a break from the trivial round, the common task. Things like

153

making love to Cynara for instance.

He had got himself curled up into a ball like a defensive hedgehog in an attempt to avoid being kicked in a vital spot. But there were no spikes on his back and it was a practical impossibility to guard all vital spots by the expedient of curling up. There was the head for example. You could sustain a lot of nasty damage in that area from a vindictively aimed toecap; and there seemed to be a large amount of vindictiveness swilling around.

It came rather as a surprise, therefore, to discover that Guayama was no longer giving him the full treatment. He put in a couple of concluding stabs with the shoe, but they were of no more than token strength and inflicted only moderate pain. And then he stopped altogether and stood back, gazing down at his prisoner in silent contemplation.

Grant waited in expectation of another attack; he felt sure that Guayama was simply taking a breather before getting stuck in again. But nothing came, and when he looked up he saw that the man was actually grinning. So maybe he was not in the killing mood; or maybe he had had orders from Velasco to keep his prisoners alive.

'You one goddam bloody fool,' Guayama said, but without anger. 'You know that?'

'I know it,' Grant said. Anything to humour the man.

'I could kill you easy.'

Grant said he knew that too.

'I kill plenty people. Don't bother me none. Don't bother me none I kill you. But hell, I let you live. Not worth kill.'

Grant was glad he was not worth killing. He could take Guayama's contempt with far less pain than his kicking. You got no bruises or broken bones from words.

Guayama went away after that and bolted the door. He took the tray but he left the scattered food and the broken china lying on the bricks. Grant hoped he would bring another meal to replace the one that had been lost, but he did not.

The rest of the day passed slowly for Grant. His ribs were sore and he had a bruise on the side of his face where he had been struck by the tray. By nightfall he was feeling both hungry and thirsty, but he had become resigned to the likelihood that he would receive nothing more at least until the morning. Guayama was probably punishing him for the attack with the brick.

He thought about digging out another brick but decided that it was not worth the trouble. Guayama would be far too cautious to give him another chance of using such a clumsy weapon; and besides, in his present condition he hardly felt up to it anyway.

Again he fell to wondering about the girls. He had not heard the faintest sound of them, and Guayama had given him no real

155

information regarding their condition. He had dropped hints, but that was all; and perhaps the hints had been given only to torment the captive. They had done that sure enough, for though he tried to convince himself that Guayama was just playing with him, he could not help suspecting that there might be some truth in what he was saying. The man was an animal, and with no one to restrain him he might be satisfying his lust with one or both of the female prisoners. Yet there had been no screaming, so perhaps such suspicions were unfounded. He just could not be sure.

When it grew dark he sat on the cardboard and leaned back against the wall, trying to sleep. The pain in his chest did nothing to help, but he had slept little the previous night and eventually he dozed off. When he awoke he was lying on the floor and daylight had come.

He felt stiff and sore, but he got up and exercised his legs and arms, relieved to find that he was in no worse shape. His chief problem was thirst, for he had drunk nothing since the middle of the previous day and he wondered whether Guayama was going to continue with the starvation treatment.

But at nine o'clock Guayama put in an appearance with breakfast. He came in warily, but Grant was standing well away from the door and made no move to attack him. It would have been foolish to do so because, quite apart from being in much better physical condition than the prisoner, Guayama had the Luger stuck ostentatiously in his belt.

'So you're taking precautions now.'

Guayama grinned at him. He set the tray down on the floor and unloaded the plate and mug that were on it, all the while watching Grant with care. He straightened up, letting the tray dangle at his side from one hand. He looked at Grant's bruised and swollen cheek.

'Don't look so good.'

'I don't feel so good.'

'Your fault. You start things, you ask trouble.'

'I'm not starting anything else.'

'Wise man. You eat now. Soon feel more good.'

'I hope so. You think Velasco will come back today?'

'Maybe. Maybe not. You wait, you see.'

'He's gone to see Mr Harrera, hasn't he?'

Guayama laughed. 'Keep guessing, gringo.'

He went away. Grant ate the meal and would have been grateful for another mug of coffee, or maybe two; he was still thirsty. Nothing happened during the morning except a shower of rain which produced the kind of odour that comes when rain falls on dry ground. But the shower soon passed and the sun came out and the temperature in the wash-house rose. Grant felt dirty as well as sore; he fingered the two-day stubble on his

157

face and tried to figure out a better way of gaining his freedom than the one that had failed.

When the idea came to him it was so simple that he cursed himself for not having thought of it before. The roof was the way, and it had taken him as long as this to see it.

He climbed on to the brickwork in which the copper was set and found that his head was level with the rafters at the lower end of the roof. He could see that the slats were old and that the worm was in them, and he felt confident that he could break them without difficulty. His impulse was to try it at once, but he looked at his watch and saw that the time was past noon. There was a likelihood that Guayama would be coming shortly with the midday meal and it would be fatal if he were to be caught in the act of breaking the slats in the roof. So perhaps it would be best to wait until later, when Guayama had been and gone and he could count on not being interrupted while making his escape. Then, too, he might have a few hours of grace before the break-out was discovered.

It was difficult to be patient now that he saw how he could gain his freedom, and for some reason Guayama was late in coming. At half-past one he had still not been, and Grant was in a quandary, wondering whether perhaps this was another piece of starvation punishment and the man might not be coming at all, or at least not until evening. So ought he to go now? Time was slipping away and the minutes were precious. At a quarter to two he decided not to wait any longer, and he was in fact up on the copper when he heard the bolts of the door being slid back. He jumped down at once and was away from the copper before the door opened and Guayama appeared with the lunch.

'You're late,' Grant said. 'I thought you were going to starve me again.'

Guayama scowled; he seemed to be in a black mood. Perhaps he was fed up with hanging around waiting for Velasco to return. 'Damn lucky you get anything. You think this one goddam luxury hotel?'

'If it is I'd hate to try the non-luxury kind. Velasco still not back?'

'You mind you own damn business,' Guayama said.

He set the meal down on the floor and went away.

Grant felt certain that Velasco had not returned.

He had heard no sound of the car. So evidently Harrera had not yet yielded up the stuff that Velasco wanted from him. Grant found this disturbing, because if Harrera was proving hard to persuade it might result in more harm to Margarita and even to Cynara. Velasco, aided and abetted by Guayama, might work off his frustration on both of them.

159

Which made it all the more imperative that he should break out of the wash-house and do something to free the girls.

He had not yet decided how to set about doing this. He could not make up his mind whether it would be better to try to release them by his own unaided efforts or to go straight for his car, to which he still had the keys, and drive away in search of help, preferably in the shape of a few husky policemen.

There were drawbacks to both plans. If he tried the first of them he would have to tackle Guayama again, and unless he could catch the man asleep, which was unlikely, that might prove a difficult business. Guayama had shown on two occasions that he was a tough nut to crack, and he had the Luger and maybe the Beretta as well. On the other hand to take the car and get the hell out of there seemed like a pretty lousy thing to do; and it might not work anyway, because Guayama would hear the car for certain and he would surely not be waiting around after that for the police to move in. He would take the Mini, possibly making one of the girls drive it while he held a gun in her side; and by the time help arrived there would be nothing left but an empty cottage.

Grant thought things over as he made a hasty meal of the food that Guayama had brought, and he still had come to no firm decision by the time he had finished. He came to the conclusion that it might be best to get out of the wash-house first and then take it from there. When he saw how things looked from the outside he might be in a better position to judge what was the most likely course of action to bring about the desired result.

Having once again climbed on to the brickwork of the copper he reached up and lifted one of the tiles and slid it downward until he was able to get a firm grip on its upper end. When he had done this it was quite easy to tip it up and manoeuvre it through the gap between the slats. He laid it on the bricks and repeated the operation with three more tiles. There was now a rectangular hole in the roof measuring some two feet by one and a quarter, barred only by one of the slats. He gripped the slat and pulled strongly downward and it broke suddenly with a loud cracking noise, sending a small shower of woodworm dust down upon his head and half choking him.

He was alarmed by the noise, which he felt sure must have been audible to anyone in the cottage, and he stood perfectly still for half a mintute waiting to see whether Guayama would appear. But nothing happened, and he carefully broke off the jagged pieces of the slat which still projected from the rafters on either side.

He waited no longer but reached up and took a grip on one of the rafters. Then he pulled himself up until his head and shoulders came through the hole. He took a quick glance round and could see no one, so he hauled his chest on to the rafter and then a leg and a moment or two later he was stretched out on the tiles, gasping a little from the exertion but out of his prison. From there it was a drop of no more than eight or nine feet to the ground, and he crawled to the edge and let himself go.

The ground was soft and grassy where he landed and cushioned his fall. He was up in a moment and moved cautiously to the corner of the building, from where he would be able to get a view of the two cars parked in the lane. He had scarcely poked his head round the corner of the wall, however, when he heard a yell and caught sight of Guayama, who had apparently just stepped out of the cottage.

Guayama had the Luger in his hand, so it looked as though he had after all heard something suspicious and was coming to investigate. Grant drew his head back quickly and was only just in time; a bullet from the pistol took a chunk out of the wall and speeded on its way with a nasty whining sound that set his teeth on edge. He saw immediately that both his plans had gone down the drain in a dead heat; now he could neither take Guayama by surprise nor could he get to the cars without being shot. He had to come up with a new plan pretty damn quick because things were moving fast, and if he hung around letting the grass grow under his feet it might not be long before it was growing over his head.

The plan came in less than a second; under pressure the brain worked at speed. Though perhaps it was not really the brain working at all but a kind of blind instinct taking over at the wheel, the instinct of self-preservation. Without waiting for Guayama to come round the corner he turned and legged it for the shelter of the wood.

He made it to the trees not a moment too soon. He heard Guayama shouting at him to stop, and then the gun again and a bullet whipping into the timber; which was a crazy way of trying to persuade somebody to obey such an order. Grant kept going.

There was the devil of a lot of tangled undergrowth among the trees—briars, brambles, nettles, the kind of thing that was no help at all to a running man. He plunged on, getting himself stung and scratched in the process but not daring to stop because he knew that Guayama would be following. And this time he had a feeling that Guayama would not be in the business of taking him prisoner; it would be the bullet in the back of the head and curtains for one. The thicket was not wide and he was through it in less than half a minute. On the other side was a stretch of low-lying ground with gorse bushes growing here and there, and shallow stagnant pools of water with tussocks of sedge thrusting up in places like vegetable stepping-stones.

There was no cover for him in this clearing, but there was a belt of more trees on the other side, and with hardly a pause he started running towards it. He had to pass between two of the sedgy pools and there the ground was wet and spongy, so that his feet sank into it with a juicy squelching sound and tended to become stuck in the clinging mud. It was hard going and he had a burning sensation in the chest and a stitch in his side, and he just could not understand the mentality of cross-country runners who did this sort of thing for fun. Though of course it might have been a lot more fun if there had not been a swine of a Latin American hard on his heels with a Luger in his hand and murder in his heart.

He glanced back and saw Guayama come out of the trees and crouch down and take aim and fire. He was not sure where the bullet went, but it put a kick into him and he got some more speed out of his legs in spite of the mud. He reached the second belt of trees and went in among them at a stumbling run, and he hoped that Guayama would get stuck in the mud or fall into one of the pools and drown. But he knew it was unlikely; the bastard would stick on his tail and as soon as he had the chance he would send another little messenger of death out of the barrel of the Luger. So damn Guayama, damn him to hell. And damn

Herr Luger too for ever inventing the bloody gun; he should have found some more useful outlet for his blasted ingenuity.

He had gone no more than a few yards into the trees before he was out of them again. He had come to a stream which was about five yards wide and so clear and shallow that he could see the sand and pebbles of its bed. It was chattering away like a direct descendant of Tennyson's brook, but Grant had no time to stop and listen to it. He could have crossed it easily enough, but on the other side there was open ground again and he was feeling too fagged out to sprint across it. Instead, he turned and began to follow a parallel course to the little river, keeping in among the trees for cover. With any luck when Guayama came to the stream he would not know which way his quarry had gone and would go off in the wrong direction.

The stitch in his side was really hurting Grant now and he had a nasty suspicion that Guayama's kicking had given him one or two cracked ribs; there was a lot of pain down there when he breathed deeply. He had to rest for a moment, and he took cover in a clump of brushwood, crouching down so that it would be more difficult for his pursuer to see him.

For a time he could hear nothing but the murmur of the stream and the sound of a helicopter in the distance, and he began to have hopes that Guayama had indeed gone off

165

in the opposite direction. But the hopes were short-lived, for a little later he heard someone walking along the bank of the stream, and peering through the foliage he caught sight of the man approaching, the pistol still in his hand.

There was a length of fallen branch lying near where Grant was hiding. It was about one and a half inches in diameter and a couple of feet long, and it was not rotten, having probably been broken off in a recent gale. He stretched out his hand and grasped it just as Guayama drew level with the hiding-place. He seemed to have some intuition that the fugitive had gone to ground and was not far away, for he came to a halt and peered into the trees, muttering to himself. But he still seemed uncertain, and he turned and gazed across the stream as if debating in his mind whether or not it would have been possible for Grant to cross over and run fast enough to be out of sight before his own arrival at the water's edge.

Then he shook his head and turned again, peering straight at the spot where Grant was hiding.

'Where are you?' he shouted suddenly. 'Come out, you sonuvabitch. Show you damn face.'

Grant did not move. He could see Guayama and it seemed impossible that the man could fail to see him. But perhaps Guayama's eyesight was not as good as it might have been.

Nevertheless, he began to move into the wood, and the direction he was taking was going to bring him within a foot or two of the brushwood clump.

He came nearer, drew level with the clump. Grant began to think he would go past unseeing, but he did not; he came to a halt and seemed to be sniffing, as though like a real hunting animal he could detect the scent of his prey. He began to turn, and Grant guessed that he knew or sensed that he was close. The Luger was thrust forward, poking into the brushwood, and the man started to follow.

Grant jumped up and struck with the branch. The heavy end hit Guayama's wrist, knocking the pistol out of his grasp. Guayama gave a bellow of rage and anguish. He dropped on one knee, groping for the pistol with his left hand. Grant swung the branch again, hitting him on the back of the head.

Guayama had a hard skull, but the branch was harder and it had been wielded with no light hand. He pitched forward on to his hands and missed the gun. Yet he was still making an attempt to get up when Grant hit him again, and this one was for the jackpot. Guayama went down and did not get up.

Grant picked up the Luger and left him there.

CHAPTER THIRTEEN

WHO'S EDGAR?

He went straight back to the cottage, wasting no time. He went in at the front door and could see no one in the living-room. He went to the kitchen and there was no one in there either. He found the narrow twisting staircase and climbed it quickly. At the top was a tiny landing with two doors opening off it. He tried one door and discovered a bedroom with a rumpled bed and a lingering odour of cigar smoke. It was not hard to guess who had been sleeping in there.

He went to the other door and turned the knob. The door was locked and there was no key in the lock. He knocked on the door and called: 'Is anyone in there?'

Cynara's voice answered immediately: 'Oh, Sam, is it you?'

'Yes, it's me. Stand away from the door. I'm going to break it open.'

He balanced himself on his right leg and kicked the door with the sole of his left foot. There was a cracking sound and it gave a little. He planted two more kicks on it close to the lock and some of the woodwork splintered and the door flew open.

It was a very small room and much of the

space was taken up by a double bed with brass ends. Margarita was lying on the bed fully clothed and propped up with pillows. She looked pale and drawn and there was a bandage round her head. The bandage was stained with blood on one side.

Cynara had been standing by the dormer window, but as soon as Grant came into the room she ran to him, flung her arms impulsively round his neck and kissed him.

'Oh, Sam darling,' she said. 'Oh, how good it is to see you.'

'It's good to see you, too,' he said.

And then she took a second look at him and cried: 'My God, Sam, what happened to you?'

'Guayama, that's what. But it's nothing to worry about.' He knew he must be looking like something nasty the dog had brought in, but it was not important. 'The question is, what happened here?'

'You mean to Margarita?' She lowered her voice and he could detect the sense of shock she was still feeling as she said: 'That animal! He cut her ear off with a knife.'

Grant was stunned. 'Oh, my God! But why?'

'Because Velasco told him to.'

'But why would Velasco want him to do that?'

'So that he could take it to Mr Harrera, to put the pressure on him. That's where Velasco has gone.'

'It's what I guessed; and I heard the

169

screaming but I never imagined what was the cause. Christ! They're not human.' He gave her a questioning look. 'Did anything else happen? To either of you. I mean, has Guayama—' He did not finish the sentence, but she took his meaning.

'Oh, no, nothing like that. I think he had orders from Velasco. Since Velasco left we've been locked in here alone for most of the time. He's brought us food now and then, but he's behaved himself.'

Grant felt relieved. He said: 'Do you know when Velasco is coming back?'

'No; but I shouldn't think it will be long now. You say you heard the screaming. Where have you been?'

'Shut in the wash-house. I finally managed to escape through the roof, but Guayama spotted me and took a shot at me and I had to run for it.'

'So that's what the shooting was. Where is Guayama now?'

'When I last saw him he was lying under some trees by a stream. He may be dead for all I know; I hit him hard enough.'

'You did!' She looked at him with a curious expression, as though seeing something in him she had never suspected was there. A brutality to match Guayama's? But when she spoke again there was nothing but admiration in her voice and in her eyes. 'You really are a rather wonderful person, aren't you, Sam?'

170

'I don't know,' he said. Was it wonderful to thump somebody on the head with a lump of wood? 'But I think we had better get out of here at once, because if Guayama isn't dead he's maybe going to wake up with a sore napper and come back here in the devil of a rage. Not that he can do much now; I took the precaution of pinching his gun.'

'Oh, my!' she said. 'Better and better.'

Grant walked to the bed and spoke to Margarita. 'Are you feeling well enough to travel?'

'Oh, yes,' she said; and she sounded eager to get on with it. 'I'll be only too glad to be away from this place. Captain Velasco will be coming back, you know, and I don't think I ever want to see him again.'

'That's understandable.'

She was getting off the bed. 'My shoes are somewhere around, I think.'

Cynara brought them to her and helped her to put them on. She seemed to be rather unsteady on her feet and needed some assistance in going down the stairs.

When they were all in the living-room Grant said: 'We shall have to take you to hospital.'

For some reason the idea seemed to alarm her. 'No, it won't be necessary. I shall be quite all right.'

'But you must have that—' he hesitated, searching for a word—'that injury properly attended to.'

'No hospital,' she said firmly.

'Well, at least a doctor.'

But she was just as strongly opposed to that.

'Why?' Grant asked. He failed to understand her reluctance to have professional medical attention.

'A doctor would have to report it to the police, wouldn't he?'

'Well, yes, I suppose so.' Whoever treated the wound would want to know how it had been inflicted, and it was hardly the type of thing that could be passed off as an accident.

'I don't think we want the police to come into this,' Margarita said.

Grant was not sure why she was opposed to having the police involved; perhaps it had something to do with her father, or experience with the police in her own country. If it came to the point, he was not particularly keen on dragging them in, either, now that the girls were free. The police had a way of asking a lot of awkward questions.

Cynara had an idea. 'I know somebody who would do what's necessary and not make any bother.'

'Who?' Grant asked.

'His name is Peter Wilmott. He used to be a medical student until he dropped out.'

'That doesn't sound very reassuring.'

'Oh, it's all right. He knows a lot. He just decided he'd rather do something else with his life.'

'Like what?'

'This and that. His own thing.'

It sounded vague, but there was no time to argue about it. Time was precious.

'We'd better go to your place,' Cynara said. 'You can drive Margarita in the Maestro and I'll bring the Mini.'

'Don't you think we ought to take her home?'

'Not yet. We don't know what the situation is like there. We don't want this sort of thing happening all over again, do we? She'll be safe at the flat.'

Grant had to admit that there was some sense in that. He glanced at Margarita. 'Does that suit you?'

This time she raised no objection. 'If you don't mind.'

'Oh, I'm past minding,' Grant said. 'Let's go.'

They were getting into the cars when Guayama appeared. He came round the end of the cottage and across the footbridge at a shambling run.

'You stop. Stop there,' he shouted.

Grant showed him the Luger. 'No, pal; you stop.'

Guayama came to a halt, staring at the gun.

'Get going, Cynara,' Grant said.

She started the Mini and drove off. Margarita was already sitting in the Maestro. Grant slid into the driver's seat and got the engine going. Guayama came up to the window and put a hand on the door. He had a raw bruise on his head and there was a smear of blood on his face. He was angry and he was probably feeling none too well.

'I kill you,' he said. 'Sometime I kill you real good, you goddam bastard.' There was a thickness in his voice, as though the words had to be forced out past a deal of obstruction.

Grant was unmoved by the threat. 'You lost, pal. Why don't you accept it? This hasn't been your day.'

He set the car in motion. Guayama took a clumsy swipe at him through the window, missed his mark and fell to the ground as the car moved away.

'There's a man who's going to be in trouble when Velasco gets back,' Grant said. 'He's not going to like what he finds here.'

Margarita said nothing. Grant could understand how she must have been feeling. The prospect of Guayama's being in trouble with Velasco was small consolation for the loss of an ear.

*   *   *

Velasco got back to the cottage soon after eight o'clock in the evening and found Guayama waiting for him, but no prisoners. Grant had been right: he did not like it.

'You lost them! You let them get away!'

174

Guayama offered a lame explanation of how it had happened. 'It was not my fault.'

'Not your fault!' Velasco was scathing. 'All you have to do is look after two girls and an unarmed man, and you let the man get free and take your gun from you and then drive off with the women. And now you tell me it is not your fault. You are an incompetent idiot.'

Guayama scowled sullenly. 'You should not call me that.'

'I shall call you what I wish. It seems I am saddled with a dunderhead who is fit only to carve off people's ears.'

'I have done more for you than that, Captain. You have no reason to complain about me.'

'I have reason enough. Look at you. You have not even washed the blood from your face. You are not only incompetent, you are also filthy. You have the habits of a pig.'

Guayama reddened, and he clenched his fists. He would have liked to rush at Velasco and beat him to a pulp, but he did not dare. He had never been so insulted; he, Sergeant Diego Guayama; it was beyond bearing. He had served the captain well and these were the thanks he got, all because of a small error of judgement for which any man might have been excused.

Velasco's wrath subsided later. He was too pleased with the outcome of his dealings with Harrera to be in a temper for long. He even

175

had some regret for having spoken to Guayama so harshly; perhaps it had not really been the sergeant's fault that the prisoners had escaped. And it made no difference anyway, since the imprisonment had already served its purpose.

He decided to make his peace with Guayama, and he even went so far as to show him the photographs he had taken from Harrera. It was strictly against the orders he had received from Alvarez, but what of that? There was no reason why Alvarez should ever know.

'Interesting, don't you think?'

Guayama looked at the photographs and sucked his breath in sharply.

'You recognise the two people, of course?'

Guayama recognised them. His brain was not one of the quickest when it came to working things out, but it did not take him long to see what red-hot material the pictures were. For was not the lady the wife of General Zaragoza? And was not the man head of the junta which had taken over the government of his native country? There was potential dynamite in the photographs.

'It is no wonder,' he said, 'that General Alvarez wants to get his hands on these.'

'No wonder at all.'

'And of course the general will be generous in rewarding the man who brings them to him.'

'I think he will not be ungenerous,' Velasco

176

admitted.

Which was all very nice for the captain, Guayama thought. But what was he, Sergeant Guayama, going to get out of it? Not much probably. Velasco was being pleasant to him now, but he had not forgotten those earlier harsh words and he was still resentful. It occurred to him that he owed Velasco no loyalty, for he had always done more for the captain than the captain had done for him. It was he who had had to do the dirty work and Velasco who had got most of the credit.

Slowly an idea took root in Guayama's mean little brain and began to flourish. Perhaps the time had come for him to do something that would benefit himself, that would bring a reward to match the value of his work. Yes, he really did believe the time had come.

'We shall return to London tonight,' Velasco said. He gathered up the photographs and put them back in the folder. 'Tomorrow we shall leave for home.'

*　　　*　　　*

Margarita sat on a chair in the living-room of Grant's flat while Peter Wilmott unwound the bandage from her head. Cynara had gone off to fetch him in the Mini as soon as they had got back to London, and he had come at once.

Wilmott was not quite everybody's idea of a

family doctor. It was not the usual practice for GPs to go visiting with bare feet, wearing boiler suits and carrying their medical gear in surplus army haversacks. Perhaps it would have added something to the diversity of life if they had; but public confidence in the profession might have suffered.

Grant himself had no great confidence in Wilmott in spite of Cynara's assurances. He was a rather plump young man and his face was so garnished with yellow hair that it was impossible to say with any accuracy what lay beneath this camouflage. He wore large silver-rimmed glasses, and from further information supplied by Cynara Grant gathered that he made some kind of living by various means such as plucking a guitar and singing folk songs in the tunnels of tube stations and similar places of public resort. He also had a clientele for his medical services among the drifting fraternity of drop-outs and drug addicts, and practised the profession for which he had never qualified in a manner that was strictly against the law.

When he had finished unwinding the bandage he examined the place where the ear had once been and made little clicking noises with his tongue. It was the first time Grant had seen the wound and he thought it looked bad. There was a lot of congealed blood, and the part of the ear that was still joined to the girl's head had a jagged appearance, so maybe

Guayama's knife had been none too sharp or he had been clumsy. No wonder she had screamed.

'What do you think, Pete?' Cynara asked.

'I'll give an opinion when I've cleaned it up a bit,' Wilmott said. 'I suppose you don't want to tell me who did this and why?'

'I think it would be better if we skipped that.'

'Okay. It's none of my business. But next time it might be as well to use a scalpel.'

'There won't be a next time.'

'No, I guess not.'

Grant was amazed at what the haversack contained. Wilmott evidently had no difficulty in obtaining drugs, though it was unlikely that they came through the normal channels. As far as it was possible to judge, he appeared to be competent. His final verdict was that there was no cause for concern.

'It'll be okay. You'll need to keep the dressing on for a while, but it'll heal nicely. Nobody will ever see the scar if you wear your hair long.'

Margarita thanked him. 'I am very grateful to you for coming so quickly.'

Wilmott grinned. 'All part of the service.'

Grant wondered what his charge would be, but he decided to let Cynara work that out with him when she took him back to his place. She would probably drive a harder bargain than he could.

At Margarita's request he put a call through to her father. Harrera sounded relieved but not greatly surprised to hear that his daughter was safe. He began to ask questions, but Grant was too tired to go into details.

'She'll be staying at my place tonight. I'll come and see you tomorrow morning and we'll talk things over.'

He rang off before Harrera could raise any objections.

While Cynara was gone Edgar Wright turned up. She had got in touch with him by telephone and given him the address. She had also told him that Margarita had been injured but had not said in what way. As a consequence he was in a pretty worried state of mind when he arrived, and the sight of the girl with a bandaged head did very little to relieve his anxiety.

'My God!' he said. 'What happened?'

Margarita seemed embarrassed; it was not the easiest of things to tell him straight out. 'Don't look so horrified,' she said. 'I'm not dying.'

'But where have you been? Why did you go away like that without telling me? I've been out of my mind. And now this. What has been going on?'

'Don't badger her,' Grant said. 'It's a long story and she's had a hard time.'

He was contrite at once. 'Of course. I'm sorry. But I've been worried sick.' He went

180

over to Margarita and took her hand and kissed her. 'I'm just glad you're safe. You can take as long as you like about telling me what happened to you.'

She told him slowly, with Grant chipping in now and then with bits of explanation when he thought they were needed. But whichever way it was told, it was impossible to avoid eventually revealing the unpleasant fact that underneath that bandage round the head was a kind of gap where one of the ears should have been.

There was really no way of cushioning the impact and it drove Wright almost into a frenzy. 'They did that to you! Oh, my God! Oh, the filthy swine! Let me get my hands on them! Just let me get at them! I'll murder them. I'll—'

'Now cool it,' Grant said. 'You won't do anything to them because they won't be around long enough for you to do it. If you want to take revenge you'll have to go to Central America, and I wouldn't fancy your chances there.'

It took him some time to calm down, and then he started talking about going to the police and they had to get him off that, too. In the end Grant convinced him that there was nothing useful he could do except be particularly nice to Margarita, and he said that was easy because it was just what he wanted to do anyway.

'It doesn't matter a bit about the ear,' he told her. 'Not to me, I mean.' He must have realised that this sounded not quite right, and he added hastily: 'What I really want to say is that it won't make any difference to the way I feel about you. If you'd lost both ears I'd still love you just as much.'

Cynara came in as he was saying this. She said: 'I should just think so, too. I wouldn't have much of an opinion of you if you didn't. Have you thanked Sam for finding her?'

He looked a bit sheepish. 'I forgot. But I am most awfully grateful.'

'So you ought to be. He could have been killed. And look at that bruise on his face. He didn't get that playing snooker, you know.'

'I don't play snooker,' Grant said.

They had a hard time getting rid of Edgar; he wanted to stick around and guard Margarita in case Velasco and Guayama turned up.

'They're not going to,' Grant said. 'They don't know where she is.'

'But can we be sure of that?'

'I can. How about you, Cynara?'

'Me too,' she said. 'Beat it, Eddie.'

He was finally persuaded to leave at about half an hour after midnight. Grant had already fallen asleep on the sofa. Cynara woke him up to tell him that Edgar had gone.

'Who's Edgar?' Grant said, and fell asleep again.

CHAPTER FOURTEEN

IRONY IN IT

'Do you want me to drive?' Guayama asked.

They had eaten a light snack and were ready for the return journey to London. It was half-past nine and the light was beginning to fade. At first when Guayama had told him about the escape Velasco had thought of leaving immediately for fear the police might pay a visit to the cottage. But Guayama told him that the others had left fairly early in the afternoon and if they had intended going to the police there would have been blue uniforms all over the place long before this. So it looked as though the law was being left out of it. Which was all to the good.

Velasco looked at Guayama's head and face, which had been cleaned up but still appeared somewhat the worse for wear. 'I think it will perhaps be better if I do the driving. You are not in the best of shape, I would say.'

Guayama shrugged. He was not bothered either way. He got into the passenger seat of the Cavalier, and Velasco started the engine and drove away from the cottage.

'I shall not be sorry to be home again,' he said.

Guayama agreed. 'It is always good to be going home.'

They had covered some twenty miles of the journey to London and were still in the heart of the East Anglian countryside when Guayama said: 'Take the left-hand turning up ahead.'

Velasco retorted with a note of surprise: 'What are you talking about? Why should I take that turning?'

'Because I tell you to,' Guayama said; and he jabbed the small Beretta that he had taken from Margarita into Velasco's side.

'You are joking,' Velasco said. But he knew that Guayama never made jokes of that kind.

'Try not doing as I tell you and see if a bullet in the guts is any joke. Slow the car or you will not get round the corner.'

Velasco slowed the car, and when they came to the turning he took it on to the minor road that branched off to the left.

'Keep going,' Guayama said.

Velasco kept going because the gun was still very close to his side. The minor road was narrow and winding, with hedges on each side. Guayama was keeping a sharp watch for the kind of place that would be suitable for the purpose he had in mind. They came to a bridge over a small river and a few scattered houses, then a crossroads. There was a signpost, but the names on it meant nothing to Guayama.

'Straight on.'

'Have you gone crazy?' Velasco said. 'This is leading us nowhere.' But he drove on.

They passed a church, went down a slight hill, turned another corner and came to a stretch of road running between thick conifer plantations. Guayama told Velasco to take the car off the tarmac on to the wide grass verge. Velasco did so, the car bumping over the uneven ground and coming to a halt.

'Switch off,' Guayama said.

Velasco stopped the engine.

'And the lights.'

Velasco switched off the lights. There was still enough twilight remaining for them to see the dark stands of trees on either side.

'What are you going to do?' Velasco asked. He was uneasy and it was apparent in his voice.

'You'll see,' Guayama said.

He got out of the car and went round to the other side. Velasco lowered the window and looked at him.

'Now get out,' Guayama said.

Velasco did not move. 'I refuse.'

Guayama poked the Beretta through the window. 'I could shoot you and drag you out afterwards. Is that what you want?'

Velasco saw that he had little choice. He opened the door and stepped out.

'Now walk towards the trees,' Guayama said.

Velasco hesitated, and Guayama jabbed him with the pistol. 'Move!'

Velasco began to walk. Guayama kept very close behind him, touching him now and then in the back with the muzzle of the pistol to remind him that it was there.

They came to the trees and went into the plantation. There was a scent of pines and the ground was soft underfoot. Suddenly Velasco began to run. There was so little light under the trees that he had only to put a very short distance between himself and Guayama and there would be no catching him; he would be lost in the wood. Guayama was aware of this and he fired the pistol.

Velasco gave a cry but continued running. Guayama went after him and fired two more shots. Velasco staggered a few yards further and pitched forward on to his hands and knees. When Guayama came up with him he was making vain attempts to get to his feet. Guayama gave him a kick, and he fell over sideways and lay on his back staring up at the sergeant.

'You're finished,' Guayama said. 'You know that, don't you? Finished.'

'Why?' Velasco whispered. He seemed unable to understand the reason for this sudden and fatal change that had come about in his relationship with the other man. 'Why, Diego?'

'Because you treat me like a dog, always like

186

a dog. I have had enough. Now I am going to be my own man.'

'But what will you do? When you get home they will execute you. You cannot get away with it.'

'You are wrong,' Guayama said. 'I will have the pictures now and I will have the reward.'

'No, it is you who are wrong. Alvarez is my uncle; I am his favourite. He will want to know what has happened to me. He will arrest you, have you shot.'

'Alvarez will do nothing,' Guayama said.

Velasco began to plead with him. 'We have always been good comrades, you and I. You cannot do this to me. Think of all the years we have worked together, Diego.'

'I am thinking of them. All the years I have worked for you, served you. And what did I get out of it? Nothing. But now I have something and I mean to make the most of it.'

'No, no, Diego. Please.'

'Don't whine,' Guayama said. 'You are supposed to be a soldier. Try to die like one.'

He stooped and put the Beretta to Velasco's head. Velasco made an attempt to turn his head aside, to avoid the deadly muzzle of the gun, but it was impossible. Guayama pressed the trigger and Velasco gave up moving his head, gave up trying to escape his fate, gave up everything.

Guayama went back to the car and took a spade from the boot. He had found it at the rear of the cottage and had secretly taken it to the car when Velasco's attention had been elsewhere engaged. He returned to where the body was lying and began to dig a shallow grave. When it was deep enough he rolled Velasco into it and dropped the Beretta in beside him. Then he shovelled the soil on top of him, stamped it down and levelled it as far as possible. He gathered some brushwood and scattered it over the grave as camouflage and took the spade back to the car. When he had driven part of the way to London he got rid of the spade by dropping it in a ditch.

*   *   *

Grant drove out to the Hampstead house in the Maestro, leaving Cynara with Margarita in the flat. Margarita had suggested that she should go home now, but Grant had persuaded her that it might not be wise.

'We don't know quite how things stand. With Velasco and Guayama still around there's no sense in taking any unnecessary risks.'

Cynara agreed. 'Let Sam talk to your father first. And besides, Pete said he would drop in and see how you're getting on.'

'I'm fine,' Margarita said.

'Well, don't push it. There's no hurry.'

It was getting on for eleven o'clock when Grant arrived at Harrera's place, and he found the man waiting for him with some impatience.

'I was expecting my daughter to be with you,' he said.

'She would have come but I thought it would be better if she didn't—just for the present.'

'How is she? Has she had medical attention?'

Grant assured him that his daughter was well and that she had had her injury attended to. He did not think it necessary to give a description of the medical attendant; it might have destroyed Harrera's confidence in the kind of treatment Margarita was receiving.

Harrera wanted to know how it came about that Grant had been involved in the rescue of his daughter. Grant told him.

'So you did not believe me when I told you she was touring in Europe?'

'No. It seemed unlikely that she would have gone there without mentioning it to Edgar Wright.'

'I suppose so. But you and Miss Jones should not have interfered. It was not really any of your business.'

'Perhaps it was lucky we did. Those men might still have been holding Margarita hostage if we hadn't.'

Harrera shook his head. 'That is most unlikely. They would have released her as soon as Velasco got back to the cottage.'

'What makes you think that?'

'He gave his promise. And there was no longer any need for them to keep her. I had given him what he wanted from me.'

'Oh, I see.' Grant felt a sense of deflation. He might have saved himself a deal of trouble and injury if he had known. Now it seemed that all he had done had been without purpose, since Harrera had already given in to Velasco's demands. 'You are right,' he said. 'We should not have interfered.'

'But you did,' Harrera said. 'And please don't think I am ungrateful. At the moment it is difficult to express my feelings. I have had a shock, a terrible shock. You cannot imagine—'

'I think perhaps I can.' Grant guessed that he was referring to the severed ear. 'But it's all over now. When Margarita comes home—'

Harrera interrupted him. 'It is not all over. That is where you are wrong. The threat remains.'

'The threat?'

'To my life. It is what this whole sorry affair has been about. Now we are back to where we started; the situation is unchanged and my daughter has been mutilated for nothing.' Harrera's tone was bitter. 'And the irony of it is that if I had known what you were doing, Mr Grant, there would have been no need for me to relinquish my shield.' He made a gesture of annoyance. 'But why say that? Perhaps after all it never really was a shield; perhaps in fact I did not need one. And perhaps now I do. Yes, there is certainly irony in it.'

Grant was not quite sure what Harrera was telling him; possibly he was simply thinking out loud. One thing was certain; he was not a happy man; he looked old and tired and broken. But there was nothing more that Grant could do for him, and he made an excuse and took his leave.

When he arrived back at the flat he was able to assure Margarita that she no longer had anything to fear from Velasco and Guayama.

'Your father gave Velasco what he wanted and I wouldn't be surprised if they're already on their way home.'

He had the impression that she heard the news with mixed emotions; she seemed happy yet sad.

'So he gave in?'

'He had no choice. Velasco knew what would persuade him. I don't think he hesitated, but I imagine there was some inevitable delay in completing the business; that would be why Velasco was away so long.'

'So he did that for my sake.'

Grant looked at her in surprise. 'Did you think he might not?'

'I wasn't sure. I couldn't be. Now I know and I am glad. But for him I am afraid.'

'You think his life really is in danger?'

'His enemies are still alive and they know now where he is.'

'Don't worry,' Cynara said. 'Things will turn

191

out all right; you'll see.'

Margarita gave a rather wan little smile. It was evident that she was far from convinced that they would.

*　　　*　　　*

Valesco and Guayama had entered the United Kingdom on forged passports. Bearing in mind the kind of mission on which they were embarked, it had been deemed advisable to provide them with false identities. Guayama, seated in a jumbo jet several thousand feet above the Atlantic on a flight from London to Miami, was again travelling on his unofficial document. Velasco, on the other hand, was travelling nowhere. Or if he was, the journey was of that terminal kind for which no papers were required and a forged passport would have been of no use to him whatever.

Guayama was feeling highly self-satisfied. He felt that he had done an extremely good job of work in disposing of Velasco; with any luck the body would not be discovered for a long time; perhaps never. And even if it was found in the next few days and the finger of suspicion was pointed at him, he would be safe; for by that time he would have a powerful protector, and there was no way the British police were going to winkle him out from the sanctuary of his native country.

He felt no remorse for killing Velasco; the

man had used him for years and had finally insulted him in the most outrageous manner. Even if there had been no advantage to be gained by hastening Velasco's departure from this world, it would have been a matter of honour to do so. Guayama, who was perhaps the most dishonourable of men, made a great issue of honour in his own mind; it justified his action all along the line.

Not that lack of justification would have deterred him from taking that action; the profit to be gained would have been motive enough. And it had not taken him long to recognise the possibility of much profit for himself when Velasco had shown him the photographs. Velasco had been a fool to do that; but no doubt he had been so pleased with himself for having got them that he simply had to show them to someone, just to demonstrate how clever he had been.

But not so clever really. Oh, no, not at all clever when it came to the point. Guayama was the clever one; there could be no doubt about that now. It was Sergeant Diego Guayama who would come out of this affair with advantage, not Captain Alberto Velasco. For it was Sergeant Guayama who was flying back alone, and it was he who now had in his possession the valuable batch of photographs portraying in such revealing detail the goings-on of General Bernardo Alvarez and the lovely Señora Roberta Zaragoza.

When he thought of those photographs and pictured them in his mind's eye Guayama could not avoid uttering a rather loud chuckle, which caused the passenger sitting next to him to glance at him in slightly startled inquiry.

Guayama stopped chuckling and composed his features. The big airliner flew on towards Miami, at which point Guayama would transfer himself to another, smaller plane that would take him to his own country and the reward he felt certain was waiting there for him.

CHAPTER FIFTEEN

MAN OF HONOUR

In the course of his career in the army Guayama had never had any personal contact with General Zaragoza. Nevertheless, he knew him well enough by sight to recognise that the man standing with his back to the room and staring out of the tall window at the broad stretch of well-watered lawn outside was indeed the general.

Zaragoza had not turned his head when Guayama was shown in; he had merely dismissed the servant with the smallest gesture of the hand, so that Guayama was left standing on the sumptuous carpet just within the room and feeling more than a little nervous and uneasy in those surroundings, in spite of a determination not to be overawed.

It had not been easy to find Zaragoza. He had gone first to the barracks, but Zaragoza had not been there; then he had gone to the Military Club and had drawn another blank; and finally he had tried the general's private residence, a palatial white stone building with an extensive estate, some ten kilometres out of town. Even then, though it was admitted by the servant that General Zaragoza was at home, it had been difficult to gain admittance. But he had refused stubbornly to go away and had at last succeeded in his object; he was ushered into the presence of the great man and left there stranded on the carpet.

The room reflected Zaragoza's vast wealth; it was large and lofty and was furnished in grandiose style. Guayama had never seen such a room, containing so many rare objects, such chairs, such sofas, such tables, such ornate mirrors and rich draperies. His eyes were dazzled. And this was only one room of many, and perhaps one of the least splendid. All this squeezed from the sweat of the peasants.

Zaragoza turned at last and fixed Guayama with a baleful eye. The sergeant quailed slightly but stood his ground, taking courage from the thought of what he had in his possession.

'Sergeant Guayama,' Zaragoza said, 'I am

not in the habit of giving private interviews at my own residence to any soldier who cares to come along. I have agreed to see you only because I have been assured that you are carrying something of extreme importance to me. I hope for your sake that that is the truth.'

'It is,' Guayama said; and his voice was hoarse. 'You may be sure, General, that I would not have come otherwise. I know my place better than that.'

'Very well, then. Let us get on with it. What is this thing of great importance that you have for me?'

Guayama began to have some misgivings, to wonder whether after all he had been wise to kill Velasco, to take the photographs and bring them to Zaragoza. He even felt a touch of fear. Zaragoza was a man of honour and also a jealous man; and he, Guayama, was not only about to tell him that his honour had been besmirched but also to produce visual evidence that he was a cuckold. Was it safe to do so? Far away in England it had seemed to be; all through the long flight home it had continued to seem so; but now, face to face with the dishonoured man himself, it appeared a considerably less advisable thing to do.

He hesitated, and Zaragoza exhibited growing impatience. He glared at Guayama.

'Come along, man. What are you waiting for? What have you got?'

Guayama saw that it was too late to turn

back. He had come so far and must go on, whatever the consequences. He reached into his pocket and hauled out the folder.

'This.'

He did not hand the folder to the general but carried it to a table, opened it up and took out the photographs, spreading them out for Zaragoza to see. Then he stepped back.

Zaragoza walked heavily to the table and examined the prints. He looked at them for quite some time, and though his expression did not alter a dull red flush crept up his thick neck and suffused his face.

Guayama waited on tenterhooks, fearing some vast explosion of rage which might vent itself on him as the only human object in sight. But no explosion came. Zaragoza straightened his back, turned and looked at Guayama.

'Where did you get these?'

'From Captain Velasco. We were sent by General Alvarez to England to obtain them.'

'So. And where is Captain Velasco now?'

'He is dead, General.'

'You killed him?'

'Yes, General.'

'Why?'

'Because it did not seem fitting to me that these pictures should go to General Alvarez. It seemed to me that there was only one man who had the right to possess them, and that man was the husband of the lady. It was a question, as I saw it, of honour.'

'Honour, yes.' Zaragoza's basilisk eyes seemed to bore into Guayama's head, searching inside it for the truth. 'You killed Velasco for the sake of honour?'

'Yes, General.'

He knew that Zaragoza did not believe him. How was it possible to deceive such a man?

'What reward do you expect?' Zaragoza asked bluntly.

'No reward, General. Nothing.'

'You have done this out of the goodness of your heart, perhaps?'

'Yes, General.'

Zaragoza made an explosive sound with his lips which startled Guayama. 'Do you take me for a fool, Sergeant? You did what you have done in the expectation of a reward. Perhaps also because of a grudge against your captain, but certainly for money. Now tell me how much you wish me to give you.'

Guayama moved his feet uneasily. 'I leave it to your generosity, General.'

'So be it. You shall have your reward.'

Zaragoza walked to a picture which swung out on a hinge to reveal a wall-safe. He twisted the dial of the combination lock and opened the safe. From it he took some bundles of paper money. He came back and handed the money to Guayama.

Guayama took the bundles. He saw that the notes were of high denomination and new.

'Thank you, General.'

'It is enough?'

'You are very generous.'

'You had better count it.'

'It is not necessary, General.'

'But I insist. Go to the table and count it.'

Guayama walked to the table; it was an order. He put the bundles on the table and began to count the money.

He heard Zaragoza say: 'The reward is in two parts. The money is one part and this is the other.'

Guayama turned and saw the pistol in Zaragoza's hand. He knew for certain then that he should not have brought the photographs to Zaragoza, simply because the general was indeed a man of honour.

*   *   *

The two servants who had heard the shots and come running to the room were aghast to see the body of Sergeant Guayama lying on the carpet, some blood-stained money still clutched in his lifeless hand.

'Take this garbage,' Zaragoza said, 'and throw it on the nearest dunghill. The fool would have robbed me.'

Already the photographs had gone from the table.

*   *   *

Señora Roberta Zaragoza was astonished when her husband walked into the bedroom without ceremony. She was suffering from a headache and was lying down with the curtains drawn to keep out the harsh daylight which was trying to her eyes. Zaragoza showed no concern for the sensitivity of those lovely eyes; he switched on the electric light so that there should be no shadows in which to hide.

'Mateo!' There was a protest in the señora's voice, but in her heart there was a small tremor of alarm. 'Mateo, what is it?'

Ever since that fateful day in the Bahamas when that horrid little man had sneaked into the garden with his camera Roberta had not felt easy in her mind; there had been a threat hanging over her existence. Yet as the days passed, and the weeks and the months, and nothing dreadful occurred, no terrible exposure, she began to breathe more freely. Perhaps the photographs had been failures, had been out of focus, had been lost, destroyed; perhaps there had not even been any, for it was possible that the man had been disturbed before he had had time to do his wretched work.

It had been the end of her relationship with Bernardo. They had both had a shock and there had been a mutual agreement that, passionate though their affair had been, it simply was not worth the risk to continue with it. It might already be too late; the damage had perhaps been done; but at least they would tempt fate no more.

And then there had been the military coup and General Alvarez had become head of the new government, and he would have had little time, even if there had been the opportunity, for further dalliance with the wife of his chief confederate. Roberta had almost succeeded in convincing herself that all was well and that nothing would now come of that unfortunate incident; for surely if the man had had the photographs he would have used them long ago. But she had never been completely successful in persuading herself that all was well; still there had been the shadow of a doubt lurking like some hideous spectre in the background and ruining her peace of mind.

So when Zaragoza came bursting into the bedroom she felt that tremor of alarm; and when she looked into his face she knew that there was reason to be afraid. She sat up, propping herself up on one elbow. Her abundant dark hair was a trifle disarrayed by the pillow, but she had not been asleep and her eyes were clear. There were a few small lines about her face, scarcely visible in any but the harshest light, which betrayed the fact that the years must pass and take their toll even from the most adorable of women; but she was still beautiful and her body was almost as lissome as ever.

Zaragoza came to a halt at the side of the

bed. 'I regret this intrusion on your privacy,' he said heavily. 'I know how greatly you value it. You have always been a most fastidious person, have you not? A person scarcely able to bear the gross touch of a male animal for fear of contamination. Am I not correct, my dear?'

She stared at him and wondered whether he had been drinking. There was a kind of intoxication in his eyes. Or was it madness? His words were strange, but she supposed he was referring to the many times when she had declined his caresses, his clumsy love-making, pleading tiredness, indisposition, anything to avoid sensual contact with that no longer young and altogether repulsive body.

'I don't understand,' she said. 'What are you trying to say, Mateo?'

'What am I trying to say!' Zaragoza paused, searching for words, breathing hard. 'I am saying that you are not what you seem, what you would have me believe. You are not a squeamish person, recoiling from the least suggestion of indelicacy, of sensuality, of vice. No, my lady, you are willing enough to wallow in such things when it suits you to do so. What am I trying to say? I will tell you. I am trying to say that you are a whore.'

The final word was spat out with such venom that she recoiled as if from a blow. For a moment she was speechless, but she had been stung by the verbal attack and goaded into retaliation.

'You have no right to call me that. What madness has got into you? Have you taken leave of your senses? A whore! What possible reason can you have for making such a ridiculous accusation? I am your wife.'

'My wife, yes. Certainly you are my wife; oh, most certainly. A very loving wife.' Zaragoza spoke with bitter sarcasm. 'But you are another man's mistress.'

'I am not. It is a lie.' She flung out the denial as a kind of automatic response to the accusation. She could do nothing less. 'What evidence have you to support this slander?'

'Evidence, lady, evidence!' Zaragoza thrust a hand in his pocket and pulled out one of the photographs that Guayama had brought. It was the most explicit of them. He pushed it at her with a kind of stabbing movement of the hand. 'There is all the evidence that is needed. Do you recognise yourself? Do you recognise the man? You are not, I hope, going to say that it is I.'

She looked at the photographs and knew that the shadow had taken substance and was no longer in the background. And there was nothing she could say; denial would be futile; the proof was in Mateo's hand.

'It is a good photograph, don't you think?' Zaragoza said. 'Perhaps you would like to have it framed to put by your bedside. Or enlarged, perhaps.'

'Don't taunt me,' she pleaded. 'It was just foolishness and it was finished a long time ago. I don't know how you got this photograph, but—'

'It was brought to me with a number of others by a certain Sergeant Guayama. He thought I would pay him for them. I did—with bullets.'

'You killed him?' She had heard the shots, but only faintly, and had thought nothing of them. Now she was appalled. And afraid.

'Yes,' Zaragoza said, 'I killed him. Can you give me any good reason why I should not kill you?'

She shrank away from him. 'You wouldn't.'

'A whore would deserve no less.'

'But you are wrong. It is not what you think. Surely you can forgive one fault, a single moment of weakness, always regretted.'

'A single moment!' He flourished the photograph. 'Does this look like a single moment? This was no accidental meeting between you and Bernardo; it was planned; it had to be. When? Where?'

'Long ago. Before the junta came to power. It was in the Bahamas.'

'Ah!' Zaragoza was searching in his memory, and not without result. 'That time when you were supposed to be in Paris with your cousin. But you were not; you were taking your pleasure with that libertine. Laughing at the old fool who had married you, given you

204

everything.'

'It is finished,' she said.

'Yes, finished; that is certain.' Zaragoza dropped the photograph and seized her by the throat. He still had great strength in his hands, and the insane rage and jealousy that possessed him lent added power. 'I will make it certain.'

She began to struggle, tearing desperately at his hands with her delicate fingers. It was to no avail; the grip on her throat was relentless. She flailed with her legs; her mouth opened and her tongue protruded; her eyes bulged. Then the legs stopped moving and the fingers no longer scrabbled at Zaragoza's hands. He uttered a long sigh and relinquished his grasp.

When he left the bedroom he locked the door and put the key in his pocket. He called for his chauffeur and ordered that one of his cars, the Rolls-Royce, should be ready for him in ten minutes. He chose that particular car with deliberation, since this was to be a journey of some distinction. Unique, in fact.

When he stepped into the car he was attired in full dress uniform, quite resplendent in spite of his lack of stature and his dumpy figure. His face as the sleek car negotiated in almost complete silence the ten kilometres of road that lay before it was utterly without expression. The driver had not the slightest inkling of what thoughts were passing in the general's mind, nor had he any knowledge of the purpose of the journey. But he had no need to know; his duty was simply to obey orders.

They arrived at the ornate wrought-iron gates which gave access to the grounds of the presidential palace in less than twenty minutes in spite of some delay in the traffic of the capital. There were armed guards at the entrance, but a glance at the man sitting in the back of the Rolls-Royce was enough to reassure them. The gates were opened and the car swept on.

Zaragoza had no appointment, but for a man of his importance it was not necessary; within two minutes he was with Alvarez in a private room. Alvarez was at a loss to understand what urgent business could have brought Zaragoza to see him without warning at that hour of the day and in such splendid attire. Nevertheless, he greeted his fellow officer with cordiality.

'It is good to see you, Mateo. You are looking well.' He had seen Zaragoza at a meeting of the junta two days ago, but he spoke as though they had not met for some time. He made the motion of offering his hand, but Zaragoza seemed too blind to see it. 'Are you here on a matter of any great importance?'

'To me,' Zaragoza said, 'it is supremely important. To you also, I think.'

Alvarez made a slight movement of the

head, as though scenting the faintest whiff of danger. 'Indeed?'

'It is a question,' Zaragoza said, 'of honour.'

'Yes?' Alvarez lowered his head and looked into Zaragoza's eyes, which were as hard as flint.

'It is a matter that concerns you closely, Bernardo.'

'Ah!'

'You and my wife Roberta.'

'I don't understand,' Alvarez said. But he understood perfectly and knew that this was trouble.

'Perhaps this will help you to do so,' Zaragoza took the photograph that he had shown to his wife from his pocket and revealed it to Alvarez. 'Does this remind you of anything? A holiday in the Bahamas, perhaps?'

Alvarez looked at the photograph and knew that it was indeed trouble. Yet how had Mateo got hold of it? There had been a telephone call from Alberto in London to tell him that all was well, that he had successfully completed his mission and would be returning immediately. Alvarez had relaxed, expecting Velasco's arrival hourly. But he had not come, and here was Zaragoza with one of the photographs. So what had gone wrong? Surely Alberto would not have gone to Zaragoza, would not have double-crossed his own uncle. And yet it seemed so.

'I can explain,' Alvarez said, knowing that he could not, but searching desperately in his mind for some excuse.

'There is no need,' Zaragoza said. 'This picture is self-explanatory. And if it were not, there are others of a similar nature. Perhaps nature is the appropriate word, for it is evident that you and that whore are in a state of nature.' He used the word 'whore' with a kind of angry relish, flinging it at Alvarez like a missile.

Alvarez stood perfectly still, waiting for Zaragoza to make a move, watching him closely. 'What do you intend to do? There is surely no need to make a great thing of this. It happened, yes; I do not deny it. But it is all finished.'

'So she said.'

'And it is the truth.'

'I don't give a damn whether it is true or not. It makes no difference to me.'

'But you will do nothing rash? Think of the harm it could do politically if this affair were to be made public property.'

'You are suggesting I should let it pass, turn a blind eye, carry on as if nothing had happened?'

'It would be the wisest course to take.'

'It would not be the honourable course.'

'You are not proposing that we should fight a duel? That would be too ludicrous.'

'I agree; it would be ludicrous. But I have

no intention of fighting a duel. I have, however, every intention of killing you.'

Alvarez was amazed at the speed with which the pistol appeared in Zaragoza's hand. He had been half expecting it, but it came as no less of a shock. For a moment he could not move; then he made a rush at Zaragoza, hoping to wrest the weapon from him before it could be fired.

Zaragoza, icily calm now, shot him in the stomach.

Alvarez fell to the floor, clutching at the wound as if to pluck the bullet out. Zaragoza stooped and shot him through the head.

He straightened up, put the muzzle of the gun in his mouth and pressed the trigger for a third and final time.

CHAPTER SIXTEEN

MISSING PERSON CASE

The news coming out of Central America brought considerable comfort to Harrera and his daughter. The threat to his life seemed to have been removed now that his two bitterest enemies were dead.

Margarita had moved back to the house at Hampstead, since there was no reason for her to stay away any longer. The sight of the bandage round her head grieved Harrera; he blamed himself for the injury that had been done to her; and though she tried to console him with assurances that it was not his fault, he still felt guilty about it.

'It won't matter,' she said. 'I shall manage perfectly well with one good ear, and the scar will not be visible because my hair will cover it. Things could have been very much worse, you know.'

In fact, she saw one good result of what had happened; it seemed to have drawn her father closer to her; he appeared to be more aware of her existence, to treat her with greater consideration, to be no longer so reluctant to demonstrate the love he had for her.

Edgar Wright came to see her at Hampstead and was cordially received by Harrera. The prospect of having an English son-in-law was not one that he greatly relished, but for Margarita's sake he accepted it. She was bound to marry someone eventually, and it was quite apparent that she was in love with the young man, who was after all perfectly presentable.

In this respect he was entirely different from another visitor named Peter Wilmott, who was, Harrera gathered, some kind of doctor. Margarita seemed to have complete confidence in him, even though he appeared to be unable even to buy himself a pair of shoes.

As for Wright, it might be that marriage to him would be the best thing that could happen to Margarita. She would become British and probably never return to the turbulent country from which they had fled. He himself could never be truly happy in England, but he believed that she could and would.

What he could not understand was how the events in the Republic had come about. He could see only one reason why Zaragoza should have killed his wife and Alvarez and then himself: he must have seen the photographs that Mendes had taken. Yet who would have given them to him? Velasco in order to spite Alvarez? It seemed improbable. And yet it was certainly Velasco who had had the photographs. There had been no mention in the reports of either Velasco or Guayama, and Harrera had no knowledge of what had happened to them. To him the whole affair remained a mystery; but he was not bothered; however it had come about, the result was a good one as far as he was concerned and he was happy to accept it.

'Now,' he said, 'perhaps we can live in peace.'

'You will not try to go back?' Margarita asked.

He shook his head emphatically. 'No. For me that is all over and done with. I have no further political ambitions.'

She was glad; she had feared the news might

211

have given him thoughts of returning, of trying to re-establish a democratic government. And that might have been fatal. Perhaps that country over there was not ready for democracy. Perhaps it never would be.

*　　*　　*

Cynara went out to Hampstead to see how Margarita was getting on and brought back a report to Grant.

'She's doing very nicely. Her medical man is entirely satisfied with the progress she's making.'

'Some medical man,' Grant said.

'You shouldn't speak so contemptuously of Peter,' Cynara told him. 'He probably knows a lot more about the job than half the GPs that are knocking around and drawing fat salaries for dishing out pills to hypochondriacs.'

'Maybe that wouldn't take much doing. Anyway, I expect he's had more experience of the drug scene, seeing the kind of people he mixes with.'

'He deserves a lot of credit. Somebody has to look after those kids.'

'Well, I'll give him my bit of credit for that. Have you seen anything of Edgar?'

'Oh, yes; he was down there. He asked me if I knew how much he owed you for the job you did for him. He said he'd like to pay you and get it off his mind.'

212

'He knows where I live. I'll be happy to see him any time he likes to come along and bring his cheque-book with him.'

'Oh,' she said, 'he won't be coming. I told him not to be silly.'

'You told him what?'

'Not to be silly.'

'What's so silly about wanting to pay off a debt?'

'But he doesn't owe you anything; not in money, that is. You were doing what you did as a friend, not for measly profit. Weren't you?'

'Is that what you told him?'

'Yes.'

'Well, thanks very much. So I've been through all this for nothing.'

'Not for nothing. You have the satisfaction of knowing you've done a good deed.'

'What do you take me for? A Boy Scout?'

She came and snuggled up to him. 'Now don't be ratty, Sam darling. You know you wouldn't really have taken his money. You said yourself that you don't go in for moonlighting. What would Mr Peking have said if he'd found out?'

He wondered whether she was right, whether he would indeed have refused Edgar's money. Perhaps. But she might at least have given him the chance of doing so.

'You're starting to run my life,' he said. 'Do you know that, Cynara?'

'Of course,' she said. 'You need someone to

213

do it, don't you? Someone like me, that is.'

He took a long cool look at her. And when he had thought about it for a while he decided that she might very well be right at that.

*   *   *

Pedro Mendes read the news of the deaths of the generals and of Roberta Zaragoza in the *New York Times*. He was in that city mixing business with a certain amount of pleasure, as was his usual practice. He was taking in all the latest productions on Broadway and showing himself in various nightclubs and restaurants and strip joints around and about, as well as getting in a bit of sharp camera work here and there as the opportunity presented itself.

'Well, well, well,' he murmured. 'This is strange. This is very strange indeed.'

So in the end the set of photographs that was to have served as a life-preserver had instead cost the lives of three people. There was no mention of the man who had been shot while trying to rob General Zaragoza, and none of Captain Velasco, so Mendes had no way of knowing that the tally of fatalities was in fact five. He did not doubt that it was the photographs that were at the root of the business, and when he got in touch with Garcia on the telephone he received confirmation of this. Garcia seemed to know a lot more about the matter than had been revealed in the New

214

York papers, and he guessed that Mendes had somehow been involved.

'You're a clever one, Pedro,' he said. 'What do you get out of this?'

'Nothing,' Mendes said sharply. 'What are you talking about? Do you think it is my doing?'

'It isn't?'

'Certainly not. What a suggestion. Do you know the name of this man you say was shot trying to rob General Zaragoza?'

'Yes. He was apparently a Sergeant Diego Guayama. Notorious for brutalities in the fighting against the guerrillas. Plenty of people will be glad he's dead. Odd that the shooting should have happened immediately before Zaragoza strangled his wife and then went off to deal with Alvarez.'

'Yes,' Mendes said. 'Very odd.' And he rang off.

But the answer was quite obvious to him. Guayama had been the go-between, the bearer of the fatal pictures; though a curious one to choose. Yet it was a strange business all round; for who would have expected the former president, Señor Carlos Harrera, to make use of the photographs in that particular way?

'But there can be no doubt,' he mused, 'that the generals treated him very badly, and even a man of his elevated principles may not be above extracting a small piece of revenge when he sees the chance to do so.'

*   *   *

Mr Alexander Peking seemed pleased to see Grant when he presented himself at the office in Blunt Street, that narrow, sunless thoroughfare in the City.

'Ah!' he said, seated, massive and bearded, behind the polished expanse of desk in his inner sanctum. 'I see you have returned. I trust you had an enjoyable vacation.'

'It had its moments,' Grant admitted.

'No doubt, no doubt. Is that a bruise on your cheek?'

'It was. It's almost gone now.'

'Sustained in the course of some riotous pastime, I imagine.'

'Something of the kind.' It had certainly passed the time and it might well have been described as riotous if a few more people had been involved. 'Have you anything for me?'

Mr Peking glanced at the pad on his desk. 'As a matter of fact there is something that's just come in. Interesting assignment. I think you'll like it.'

'What is it?'

'Actually,' Mr Peking said, 'it's right up your street. It's a missing person case.'

'Oh, no, not that,' Grant said. 'Anything but that. They're poison to me. Don't you think you could let me have another week's holiday? I'm not feeling too well.'

216